FOCUS ON FRAUD

A PARKER PHOTOGRAPHY COZY MYSTERY

SUZANNE BOLDEN

LAUGHING DEER PRESS

CONTENTS

Chapter 1   1
Chapter 2   14
Chapter 3   25
Chapter 4   33
Chapter 5   39
Chapter 6   45
Chapter 7   52
Chapter 8   60
Chapter 9   66
Chapter 10   72
Chapter 11   84
Chapter 12   93
Chapter 13   103
Chapter 14   112
Chapter 15   118
Chapter 16   131
Chapter 17   139
Chapter 18   148
Chapter 19   159
Chapter 20   164
Chapter 21   170
Chapter 22   176
Chapter 23   181
Chapter 24   185
Chapter 25   196
Chapter 26   204

The end	211
About the Author	213
Also by Suzanne Bolden	215
Also by Suzanne Bolden	217

I put my arm around Aunt Ruth's shoulder as we stood side by side on Main Street. "Here we go, Auntie. You've passed the family torch off to me and I want to make you and Dad proud."

Ruth smiled up at me. "You already have, Jackie. I'm so proud of the photographer you've become and the world-famous business brand you've created. I know your father is smiling down at us."

She looked at the sign hung today as the last touch to the new Parker Photography storefront. "What our family created lives on, and I couldn't be happier you are taking it into the future. Now we'd better get ready for the grand opening." She bent down to pat my dog, Libby. "Come on, girl, let's get this party started."

Yesterday we did the obligatory ribbon cutting ceremony with Patti Hunt, Harmony's village administrator, and our local Chamber of Commerce representatives. Stuart Walters captured images of the event that would make it into the Harmony Hills Happenings Tuesday edition, along with photos from tonight's grand opening celebration. Stu was editor, reporter, and owner of the twice weekly newspaper and a huge advocate for the village. He and his wife Kim, a local realtor, would be here tonight.

Several of my friends from Chicago arrived yesterday for the ribbon cutting to support me in my new endeavor. I loved them for it. They were staying at the Riverview Motel and Cottages owned by my friend Wanda Mathis. We'd all, including Wanda, slipped away to the Wildwood Supper Club and had a lovely evening together. Having friends finally meet from the two places where I had homes was uplifting. It made my expanding world seem somehow smaller.

Chicago friends were still wrapping their heads around me setting up a second home in the village I grew up in. Ah, the comments I heard when I first told them of my plans...

In your sixties, you pick up and move to a little rural town?

Where on earth will you find good restaurants?

You have so many friends here in the Windy City!

Won't you miss your loft view of Lake Michigan?

I smiled and responded to everyone about how I considered this move forward looking.

There are great restaurants in Harmony.

I'm keeping my loft in Chicago.

I still have a water view, the Wisconsin River.

But now, on to the party!

Inside, our caterer had completed her setup. Not only was Patti Hunt the village administrator, but she was also expanding on her love of gardening and cooking by picking up side jobs catering special events. I was more than happy to give her this one, as she was also the mother-in-law of my employee, Mandy Drake. Her husband, Charlie, an attorney in nearby Greensville, was helping Patti out tonight. He was passing hors d'oeuvres around to the arriving guests.

Moveable gallery walls held not only my photography, but that of other photographic artists as well. I was so happy with the way the place looked for its grand opening gala!

I joined a couple of city friends who were stepping into the studio. "This place looks amazing! Way to go, Jacqueline," Celeste said.

Felicia agreed. "And what a quaint little town. We walked along the riverfront this morning. Cute marina. Plus, we ate lunch at a retro diner. They did an outstanding job, making it look like a blast from the past. Even a waitress named Dolly. Can you believe it?"

"Retro diner? Oh no! You were at the Harmony Diner. It has looked the same for forty-some years. And Dolly is just, well... Dolly! What you see is not fake. That's how she's always been. You are just too young to remember that."

Felicia clapped her hand up to her mouth, and Celeste laughed. "Put your foot in that one, didn't you?"

"Oops, sorry," Felicia said. Then, as a quick distraction, she asked, "You have Ethan's work here, don't you? I can't wait to see it."

"His photographs are along the wall by the stairs. I love what he sent over," I said.

Jeff Mathis, Wanda's cousin, had just arrived, and I knew I wanted to welcome him. This type of event was out of his comfort zone. "Now, if you'll excuse me, I need to say hello to some people. Enjoy yourself."

Celeste's eyebrows went up as she ran her tongue across her lips. "If you are saying hello to that Jeff Bridges lookalike hunk by the door, I'll help you," she said.

I waved her off. "Later, Celeste. Cool down."

Jeff saw me coming across the room. I could see the relief flood through him. "I was supposed to meet my cousin Wanda here, but she's going to be late. Happy for you, Jackie. Place looks great." He pointed toward one of the front windows. "I'm glad you kept that front window the original size."

The storefront glass was shattered the last time I was in town. I had my suspicions that someone threw the rock in anger, thinking I was a big city intruder trying to fancy up the town. But that was far from the truth. I loved Harmony as it was.

"Me too. It's the right fit for the streetscape, just like it has been for decades. Police Chief Mathis, seeing as you're off duty tonight, I hope you'll have some of Patti's appetizers and a beer from Stone Mill Brewery."

"Well, look at you! Way to go. Promote local. I like that," he said, giving me one of his disarming grins.

Guests kept arriving. I was grateful for their support.

A reporter from Chicago, Todd Baldwin, was here at my request. Todd's work covered social sections of newspapers, blogs, and social media. I didn't even know all the ways he helped publicize things, but I knew he was good at it. I appreciated him showing up, as I wanted to help promote the village of Harmony along with my place. "Todd, how nice to see you. I'm so grateful you came," I said to the tall, well-dressed young man with a camera hanging around his neck.

"I'm so glad you invited me JP. This'll be a great article and just in time for the summer family travel blogs. What a cute little town. And this place…" He looked around the studio, "…is perfect to showcase your work. Congratulations on what appears to be a successful grand opening."

"Did I tell you I grew up here?"

"Hometown girl makes good. That's a great storyline. I love it JP."

"Todd, I know you came here because you've covered my work before. But this time, I'd love to have you include the beauty of this area. It's called the Driftless Region."

"Driftless like the teenager living in his parent's basement?"

"Goodness no! It's a geological term."

Todd opened his notepad, pen poised above it. "Let me catch that. Driftless?"

"Yes. The last continental glacier bypassed this area, so we don't have the drift, which is silt, gravel, and sand that a retreating glacier normally leaves behind."

"Interesting name. Never heard of that. I will mention it in my writings."

"And the area has all these picturesque forested hills and stunning bluffs rising above the Wisconsin River."

I hoped my push to promote Harmony like this didn't come back to bite me. I loved it as it was, but change is inevitable. Now the village teetered on the edge of a new future. If they managed it right, they could have the best of both worlds, small town vibes and economic prosperity.

"Excuse me. I need to mingle a little. Enjoy yourself and I'll catch you later. Are you staying in town for the evening?" I asked.

"I'm staying for a couple of days, actually." He pulled out his phone and scrolled through some emails before holding it up. "At this place on Oak Street, the Whitlow Bed and Breakfast. Do you know it?"

"Hmm… no, I'm not familiar with it, but I know Oak Street well. We had a home there. It's lined with stately old houses, mostly those of the successful business owners like the lumber barons. Looks like a wonderful choice for your stay. Can we get a coffee before you leave?"

"I'd be happy to. Call me in the morning and we'll meet up. Now go enjoy your party!"

I noticed that not only Patti's husband Charlie but also her son Matt were helping serve drinks and appetizers. Patti's workspace was in my remodeled kitchen upstairs. As she came down with more small plates for the guests, I gave her a quick thumbs up. The place was filling up, and it looked like Patti would have a busy night.

Outside on the sidewalk, I'd set up a few tables and

chairs alongside the colorful flowers in their large earthenware pots. I wanted to give the guests some mingle room in the balmy evening air.

Also on a display easel outside were photographs from a local artist, who was the granddaughter of one of my aunt's friends. The young lady was chatting with Aunt Ruth's gal gang from Shady Pines. She did a nice job with her display and I noticed she had a basket of her photographs to sell. They were neatly matted and ready for framing. I know Mandy had helped her with that, which was so nice.

I stepped outside to see if she needed anything when I heard someone calling my name. "Jackie!"

Without turning around, I knew who it was.

"Jackie, what an event you've thrown here!"

"Thank you, Kim. You look gorgeous tonight." Kim Walters, wife of Stuart, was always so pulled together. I caught myself up short though, remembering the exception when she was under arrest. I smiled inside. She rebounded well. Nothing much got her down. Kim, our local realtor extraordinaire, was on top of her game tonight. She'd come with Alan Morris, the developer of The Hills, a local resort project being built in the hills above town.

"Alan, I'm so happy you made it here for the opening," I said.

Alan gave me a quick hug. "I wouldn't have missed it. I've been staying in a Riverview Motel cottage. The Hills Resort construction is coming along and it's in a phase where it needs a little hands-on attention."

Kim said, "Jackie, Alan and I wanted to talk to you about a promotion we'd like you to be involved with. We want to hit the Chicago, Milwaukee, and Minneapolis markets."

"Sounds good."

"Perfect," Alan answered. "Could you meet us at the job site tomorrow morning around 10:30?"

"Working on Sundays?"

"No rest for the wicked. I see Todd Baldwin is here. I'd like to say hi to him. Maybe get some free publicity," Alan said with a wink. "See you tomorrow."

Kim watched Alan walk away. "I wonder how he got that limp. Maybe a combat wound? Hmm... I don't know if he was in the service. An accident? Oh, whatever," she muttered, letting out an enormous sigh. "I don't know why I think these random things. Some days it is all too much. I need to focus."

I got a kick out of Kim. She could talk at length about anything. I suppose that helped her in her business.

She turned back to me and gave me a conspiratorial

smile. "I'm glad you'll work with us. This will really help me out."

"Is Stuart here tonight? I saw him at the ribbon cutting earlier."

"Now, what do you think? Of course. This opening will probably be the front page on my hubbie's Tuesday paper. When we get the promo going and the buyers arrive to view the models, I must have him put together an entire What's Happening in Harmony brochure. Yes! A special edition to attract vacationers here." Her eyes lit up. "Like this place. And Sutton's Antiques. And Taliesin and the Harmony House Museum and the marina. Oh, it'll be wonderful, and everyone will want to buy ads for it." She touched my arm and leaned in toward me. "He could use the ad revenue, I can tell you."

She stood back and flicked her fingers through her long chestnut hair, so a portion of it curled around her shoulder. Adjusting the collar of her cream silk blouse, she licked her lips, put on a smile, and disappeared into the crowd. Gotta love her enthusiasm.

I noticed Wanda arrive. She joined my Chicago friends, who had cornered Jeff. He seemed to have gotten over his social awkwardness and was totally enjoying the attention.

"Jackie, isn't this just the best?" Mandy said as she took an appetizer from the tray her husband Matt carried. "And you have the cutest servers," she said, giving him a peck on the cheek.

"Hey! No flirting with the help," he said. "And don't wobble me. Carrying these trays is a delicate balancing act."

They are such a cute couple, I thought. "Mandy, the evening is a success. I appreciate all you did to pull this together."

A blush rose to her cheeks. "Thanks, it was fun. I'm just grateful that you asked Patti to cater. She's having a blast handing out her business card right and left. You gave her a chance to show off her skills."

"I didn't realize she was so into cooking."

"And gardening! You should see her gardens out at the old farm. I'll bet she heads out there tomorrow. She calls it her happy place."

"I'm surprised Scott isn't here tonight."

I was not only surprised, but disappointed as well. Scott Drake did the remodeling job in Aunt Ruth's apartment upstairs, as well as the studio area down here. I really thought he'd come to see it in all its glory.

"My father-in-law is an avid fisherman like his son. He had a long-planned buddy trip to the Boundary Waters in Minnesota. Something he and his friends have been doing for like twenty years. I wish he could have been here too, though. The place looks amazing!"

"I agree. Scott did a terrific job. Oh, and I think we're getting a new job. Doing a promotional material shoot for The Hills Resort," I said.

"Nice! I've taken some framing orders, too." Mandy pointed outside, where Hannah and Mark Sutton were talking with Aunt Ruth. "Hannah has a stash of antique frames she wants me to see next week. I think the official launch of the new Parker Photography is a success!"

*A*nd it was a success! I'd locked up downstairs after everyone left, promising myself I'd do the rest of the cleanup tomorrow. Tonight, I wanted to enjoy the emerging evening stars and savor the feeling of knowing Harmony was now my base.

This second-story balcony above the photography studio was special to me. As a young girl, I watched the world go by from this perch. I was happy Aunt Ruth kept it all these years. There was a chill in the evening air and I appreciated Libby curled up against my toes. "You had a big night girl, didn't you? All that visiting. I saw you begged a few of those rumakis off my guests."

Libby sighed and adjusted her chin on the arch of my right foot.

A few doors down, I heard the jukebox at Shorty's start playing Marvin Gaye's song Mercy Mercy Me. I made a mental note to stop in one of these days. Shorty's was the first bar I'd tried sneaking into as a teenager. It was a rite of passage in those days.

"Okay, girl. Let's get my old bones to bed."

I stood to blow out the candle when I heard giggles.

High heels clicked by on the sidewalk underneath me.

Murmured words.

Saturday night kind of sounds.

CHAPTER TWO

The morning sun streamed through the new transom window Drake Construction added to my bedroom. Scott worked with me to transform the place, bringing it into the 21st century. More natural light for the interior was one of the transformations I'd requested.

Libby bumped against me, rubbing her nose under my arm. "I know what you want. I've got to do the same thing." The timer on my coffee maker clicked on as I walked by to take Libby downstairs. She did her business in the grass of my little backyard before we both headed back upstairs. I grabbed a coffee and went out to the balcony.

The streets were quiet. Families in their Sunday clothes, which had gotten much more casual than when

I was growing up here, could be seen walking to church. Anglers were heading out of the harbor to fish the river.

"Looks like another glorious day in Harmony, Libby."

Last night had been fun. The opening welcomed a new version of Parker Photography. We would do local family portraits, wedding photographs, and all the things my family did in the past, but also be a gallery for selling photographic art. Besides the framing, Mandy was working on our social presence. Like the apartment, it was another thing to be brought up to current times. Digital photography and the advent of the internet meant loads of competition for my business.

Todd called, and we agreed to meet at Murphy's Coffee Shop. I pulled on my khakis, a white scoop neck tee, and my trusty jean jacket. "You stay here Libby, I'll take you with me to the construction site later and you can run around there to your heart's content."

Aunt Ruth would open the studio at noon. She helped here by taking over on random days. It gave Mandy time off and me freedom from committing to a regular schedule, something I hadn't done for years. Though I had to laugh, thinking that with Libby in my life, I was obligated to her schedule. But more importantly, I think it was good for Ruth. To just stop working cold turkey might have been too much.

Grace Murphy was behind the counter at the coffee shop when I walked in. "Good morning, Jackie! We're excited to have you join our business community here in Harmony. And after the opening last night, I think you'll be a great addition."

"Thanks, Grace. And I'm happy to be able to enjoy your baked goods more often," I said.

"Your usual maple frosted donut? Your friend over there paid for it already."

I took my donut and coffee to a small table near the window where Todd waited. "Thanks for buying."

"You're welcome, JP. This place is great. And compared to city prices, the coffee and pastries here are a steal."

"How's the B&B you're staying at?"

"Perfect. Kay, the proprietor, is so helpful. She got me in Taliesin on short notice. Not possible today, but she pulled some strings to get me in tomorrow. It's been on my to do list ever since I saw Frank Lloyd Wright's studio in Oak Park."

"I met Kay Whitlow at a Historical Society meeting. She seems very nice."

"She pointed out a photograph on her wall of a family in front of Parker Photography. I wonder if that was you with your mom and dad?" Todd said.

"Really? I don't remember ever seeing one like that.

Isn't that odd? My father and his sister ran a photography business, but we don't have many photographs of us."

"Was your mom a housewife, as they were called back then?" Todd said. "Sorry if that's not PC."

"Don't be silly. That's what women are still called who stay home to raise a family, aren't they?"

Todd shrugged. "I'm not sure. I see stay-at-home used more, probably."

"But no, she wasn't a stay-at-home kind of woman. She ran the dress shop in town. She was so stylish and trendy. Fashion was her passion. I, however, prior to my leaving Harmony, spent as much time as I could with Dad and Aunt Ruth at the studio. My mom and I were both lucky to do what we loved."

We spent the next hour talking about my new business and who I was having exhibit over the coming months. Todd wanted as much information as he could get on other local attractions to include in his social media, which I learned included a blog with a very large following. He said he planned on walking the Mary Go Round.

"What on earth is that?" I asked.

He blew on his fingers and buffed them on his chest, obviously proud to know something I didn't. "It's a hiking trail that circles the entire town."

"I didn't know the parts of it connected all the way around."

"Kay told me some areas are unpaved, but the trail bed is laid for it. Who was this Mary they named it after?" Todd asked.

"I don't know. I'm just excited to know it's a walkable loop. Must be five or six miles long then. I can't wait to take it." I peeked at my watch. "But gotta run now. I'm meeting some future clients to see the building site for the resort and golf course. Enjoy your day here!"

A group of protestors were at the construction site gate when Libby and I approached. The camera crew from a Greensville's station was there as well. Apparently, the group thought blocking my entry would make for good video. I tried to read some of the signs they were waving in front of me, but I couldn't focus on them as I slowly rolled forward, hoping I wouldn't run over anyone's toes.

Why were they even here on a Sunday? This seemed staged for publicity, as many things are.

The long swing gate was wide open. I breathed a sigh of relief when I saw signs pointing me in the direction of the sales office. Hope the protestors didn't deter anyone from visiting the model next to the sales office.

Kim came bounding out to meet me before I could even get out of my car.

"Welcome to The Hills! Isn't it beautiful up here? I'm super excited you agreed to work on this promotion with me. Alan's up at the construction trailer right now. I'm so glad you're going to be living in Harmony." She actually did a little clapping before going on. "Things have been going so much smoother with Luella out of the picture. Oops, that sounded bad, didn't it? Our first phase is well under way. By next season, we should be up and ready. But part of that is successful promotion throughout this summer and fall and even winter. We hope to have the first homes enclosed so we can work on them during the weather you and I both know is coming."

She finally took a breath.

"Who's taken that building and zoning position?" I asked.

"Someone named Severson. Seems like a reasonable person. Not on the take, thank god!"

"Are the protestors slowing anything down?"

"Are they at the gate today? For heaven's sake. What on earth do they hope to accomplish on a Sunday except annoy any visitors to the model who might show up? But then I suppose that's how they get their message out."

"TV crew from Greensville was interviewing and taking video. I suppose for the 5 o'clock news."

"That doesn't help, but our market is not really Greensville. I just hope the larger market areas don't pick up the story." Kim stomped her foot. "Those darn protestors. What do they want? This is just progress! Come on, I'll give you a quick tour of the model before I take you around the grounds."

The rendering of the future Hills Resort complex looked impressive. It included indoor and outdoor pools, along with some onsite dining. She showed me the condo unit model for sale, an option for those who wanted to own instead of renting.

Libby jumped into my lap as I got into a four-person golf cart. She put her paws on the dashboard, eagerly sticking her head up to see where we were headed. Kim took us to a high point to view the golf course being carved into the landscape. From here, it looked like a scar on these beautiful hills. It was raw, unfinished. When completed, it would look very different.

Kim must have read my mind. "The contractor is trying to retain as many trees as practical, but it's not always easy to work around them. They are using lots of erosion control measures." She pointed to an area with straw covering it. "Landscapers will plant wild grasses to anchor the soil. The golf course is going to be striking. We're super excited to see it shaping up."

In the distance, I saw the construction trailer. It looked like a mobile home, but with very few windows and no appealing shutters or detailed trim. Just a basic style to run the operation out of.

"Now Jackie, let me introduce you to Rick Ballard, our construction supervisor. He often catches up on paperwork on the weekends." Kim elbowed me. "Gotta love a guy in a hard hat, right Jackie?" She cranked the little steering wheel, and we took a spin down the curve of the hill.

As soon as we pulled up and Kim slid to a stop, I heard heated voices from inside the trailer. A muscular young man came storming out, pushing past us.

Kim shouted after him. "Hey! Watch where you're going."

I heard him mumble some rather unpleasant words as he looked back at us with a scowl.

"What a hot head that one is!"

"Maybe this is a bad time?"

"Nah. We're good. These guys are just full of testosterone, I think. Always seem to have a harder edge than…oh say, someone like my sweetie, Stu."

Our presence here caught Alan and Rick by surprise as we stepped inside. Kim quickly filled the awkward moment by introducing me to Rick, a short, burly man with a dark beard and a deep tan.

He stepped over to shake my hand. "Nice to meet you, ma'am. Let me know if you need anything special for your work. Kim knows where to find me. Now if you'll all excuse me. I've been given extra work to do." He glared at Alan as he spoke.

"Rick, is the site accessible this evening? I'd like to get some sunset photos if possible. This job will take some research to get the best light. Sunset always produces such eye-catching scenes."

"Appears I'll be here late tonight, so sure. The gate will be open. Maybe Kim can leave the keys in her golf cart for you." Rick handed me his business card. "My cell is on here in case you get lost," he said with a friendly smile. "Sorry if Alan and I sounded a little gruff with each other. We're all pretty stressed. Big project deadline this week for the next draw on our construction loan."

Alan quickly interrupted Rick by saying, "No need to bring all that up on this beautiful Sunday. Jackie, let's go with Kim back into town and grab a late lunch. We can discuss what we're looking for and come to an informal arrangement about time, payment, and such. Our ad agency is excited to have the famous Jacqueline Parker as a photographer."

"We did a little name dropping, so they'd understand

how serious we are about making this an over-the-top appealing ad promo portfolio," Kim added.

"You two head out. We'll meet at the diner in an hour. Work for you?" Alan said.

"See you there." Kim took my elbow and led me back out to the golf cart. "My assistant Laura should be at the sales office now. I'd love to have you meet her."

When we were introduced, Laura said, "I believe you know my great-uncle Tom Lemke."

"Your Tom's great-niece! I'm so happy to meet you. How are he and Eleanor doing? I haven't seen them recently."

Laura grinned. "Still acting like the newlyweds they are."

"I imagine that the whole newlywed thing looks different when you're in your 80s, though," Kim said.

Laura winked. "I don't know about all that, but they are cute together. I think he has been in love with Eleanor Harmony for his entire life. And now, to be with her every day and night, even if it's mainly cuddling and holding hands, has given him a new lease on life."

"Well, I am so glad for them. Are you enjoying being part of the sales team up here?"

"I am. Kim's a great boss, and I hope I can be a realtor like her someday. With the summer coming and that big promotion you're all working on, we'll be busy. Most days are pretty quiet, but I fill that time with studying for the test for my real estate license."

"Good luck with that," I said, as I turned to leave. "Say, who was that angry young man at the construction trailer?"

I noticed Laura duck her head and turn away.

Kim looked at me and said, "Just one of the guys running the heavy equipment. Probably a problem with getting the right hours or something. Takes all kinds."

CHAPTER THREE

It had been an interesting lunch with Kim and Alan. They presented me with their ideas and plans. The ad agency they were planning to work with wasn't a Chicago one, so I didn't recognize it. The agency had given me a list of suggestions and then carte blanche to send them images of my own choosing. It seemed a little loosey-goosey to me. Most campaigns had a focus from the get-go, and a direction of how to brand things.

Kim said, "We've dipped into the budget for advertising on and off, and it's pretty low at this point."

I caught Alan shooting her a *watch what you say* look.

"Are you sure you want to hire me?" I asked. "Perhaps my fees wouldn't be warranted at this time?"

Kim said, "Oh, I'm sure. I remember seeing the

photographs of that resort in Croatia, the lodge in the ski hills of Colorado, and the Bermuda beachside retreat. Why, I just swooned when Ruth showed me those ad campaigns using your photographs. We must have you do ours. Your photographs alone will sell the place out! The images will hypnotize buyers. They will have to have one of our units. Their children will jump up and down screaming Mommy, Daddy, we want to spend summer there. Not to mention the golfers!"

"Whoa, Kim. Those promotions involved projects that were much further along than yours, so the ambiance could be captured much better. Maybe we should hold off on this for now and talk again in the future."

Alan spoke. "My understanding with Kim here, was that it would involve you with capturing the process and the progress. That this will be an ongoing ad campaign."

"I guess I didn't understand it that way. I may have misunderstood, but my impression was that it was to be a current push for summer. A start just to make some *come and see us* sort of ads, mailing, social media posts."

"Hey, that's why we're meeting right?" Kim said, obviously trying to smooth things over.

"Can you give me a contact at the ad agency handling this? I'll talk with them and see if we're on the same page," I said.

I left the meeting unsure about things. I loved the idea of working locally. It would give me an opportunity to teach Mandy more about photography. But I had to carefully evaluate the situation and how much time I should put into this job.

Right now, though, I decided to spend the rest of the day at the studio. I looked forward to seeing what Aunt Ruth thought of all the changes we'd made. Plus, I needed to spend some time feathering my new nest upstairs.

The afternoon flew by. Aunt Ruth and I packed a light supper to eat at a picnic table by the river. We enjoyed watching the river traffic and the warm summer air. I knew I'd love having more of this kind of relaxed time with her.

It was quiet by the construction gate when I pulled up an hour before sunset. The protestors were gone, but I noticed some of their hand-made signs hidden behind low shrubs, apparently for their return next weekend.

Lights were out at the model office. There wasn't any car in front. I grabbed my photography bag and tried the office door, but it was locked. Kim left the golf cart keys in the ignition, so Libby and I jumped in and started toward the Driftless golf course.

I wanted to take a few shots tonight to check on the angle of light and find views that worked with the sunset. Being in these hills, the sun would play a big part involving the horizon line changes. It could get dark quickly here, so I hurried up toward a higher point. I needed to scout for a place where the setting sun beams shot over and through the hills, casting dark shadows. I hoped to capture brilliant contrast and eye-catching drama.

I was grateful Kim had taken me around this afternoon and that I had Rick's cell phone number because things looked very different at dusk. Once I left the resort construction area, it was pretty confusing without a path or road to follow. The residential part of the project had more obvious roadbeds. I drove toward a rise in the distance, trying to steer clear of any soft looking places as I didn't want to get mired down in a mud trap.

Libby, now familiar with a golf cart, sat on the seat next to me with her paws on the dash. When I found a spot to stop, she quickly jumped down and began exploring.

Good choice, I could capture amazing shots from here. What a vista! The river reflected the setting sun.

Once the streetlamps came up in the village below, it would be amazing. Wait ten more minutes, I told myself. It will be perfect. I was at the edge of the golf course layout. The forest was relatively undisturbed here.

I called for Libby and she came charging toward me on what looked like a wild animal track or path. Probably made by deer. A squirrel caught her attention, and she darted back off into the trees.

Turning toward the view across the property, I gasped when I saw flames. It took me a breathless moment to realize I was only catching the direct sun rays bouncing off glass. How easily deceived I was! I lost sight of the fiery object. Was it a vehicle? Had it moved? Or had the sun just connected for that one moment in time to startle me?

I spent several minutes snapping photos for positioning. Enough for now. "Libby, come girl. Heading home."

Libby popped out of trees panting and ready to get back in the cart. Darn, I forgot her water. Maybe I can grab some at the construction trailer if someone is there.

I suppose it was because the golf cart was electric and didn't make a sound that the quarreling voices inside didn't stop as I approached.

I recognized Alan's voice. "Unacceptable. These

equipment purchase orders are duplicates. Unnecessary and not approved. How many times has this happened?"

"We're stuck with them, I'm afraid. Somehow two got submitted. The supplier is holding us to it."

I stepped closer to the open window. That didn't sound like Rick. It was a hesitant sounding voice.

"Alan, I don't know how this happened. Something got confused. I'll try to clear it up with them." That one was Rick's voice.

"And it better happen by the time I get back to Chicago tonight. Off the books. Out of the computer records. If my investors see one more of these mess-ups, it's bye-bye to me. And you two will be next."

The timid voice spoke up again. "Excuse me, but I'm employed by them as well and have…"

"Shut up. You're just as disposable as me," Alan said. "Now let's go through these other numbers and make some adjustments."

Rick spoke again. "Look, we can't just keep playing with numbers here. I will not be blamed for this crap. You dump it on me and then take off."

"It's your construction site, isn't it? Your fuel bills. Your equipment failures. Your delays."

"Alan, you give us next to impossible deadlines. And the inspectors are siding with the protestors over silt bags and earth slides."

"Get some better bags."

"You don't give us money for better bags. Right, Winford?" Rick asked.

Apparently, the timid voice belonged to someone named Winford because he spoke next. "Please don't put me in the middle of this. I'm just the accountant here."

"You're the keeper of the money. He's the spender of the money. I'm the getter of the money. And when I see the whites of my investors' eyes, they better not tell me there's no more to get! So, do something about it. The figures you both are showing me are wrong. They are simply unacceptable. I don't know who's been playing what with them, but I've had it."

"Sir, there aren't many…"

I expected to hear another *shut up Winford,* but there was only silence when Libby let out a *what are we waiting for* yelp. A face appeared at the window, but he didn't see me, as I was hidden in the shadows.

"Who's out there?"

I quietly tiptoed back to the golf cart before the door of the trailer opened and Alan stepped out.

"Hey Alan. Surprised to see you here. Is there water for my little Libby in the trailer? We were out taking those sunset photos and she wore herself out chasing squirrels."

Alan tried to compose himself. "Ahh…hi Jackie. You

startled us. I'm heading back to Chicago tonight and called a quick meeting to put some data together." He turned and called out, "Rick, got a thirsty dog out here."

"Thanks," I said. "It's sort of late to drive back, isn't it?"

"What?" Alan's upset was still obvious. He was distracted. "Oh, no. Not bad. Just three hours."

Rick came out with a cup of water and set it in front of Libby. He didn't look at Alan, but said, "Hold on. Winford's putting his paperwork together. He left his bicycle at the office. Can you put it in the trunk and drive him home?"

"For god's sake who the…? Tell him to hurry. I don't have all day." Alan spun on his heels and walked to his car.

"I could drop him there. I have to take the golf cart back," I offered Rick.

Rick looked at me. "No thanks, Jackie." He glared at Alan's back. "Mr. Morris can wait for him."

Alan slammed his car door, his fingers white knuckled around the steering wheel. I made a quick exit in the golf cart, holding the paper cup in my right hand while Libby lapped the water up.

This was one place I wanted out of.

Tensions were high.

What was all that about, I thought? The stress was obvious. Kim had mentioned something about money being an issue for the development, so I suppose it was putting pressure on everyone.

While driving back on the winding road toward downtown Harmony, I decided to visit Shorty's tonight. Time I met the new owners and introduced myself. Plus, a cold beer sounded wonderful.

Libby looked happy to be home. She turned two circles in her doggie bed before curling up and tucking her paws over her nose. I went down the back staircase to the alley and walked over to the tavern's back door. It opened with a squeak, startling a young man and his girlfriend playing pool on the green felt billiard table.

The light lit the table from above, leaving the rest of the room in shadows.

I walked past them and into the primary room of the tavern. Three men sat at a small table playing cribbage. They didn't even look up when I came in. A couple stood by the jukebox picking out music. Two men sat on stools watching the Milwaukee Brewers on the television above the dark wooden back bar. And who was behind the bar but the same bartender who'd kicked Wanda and I out of here as teenagers. Shorty Schuster. He had to be in his eighties. I chose a bar stool near the jukebox.

"Welcome. What can I get you, Jackie?"

My jaw dropped. "You recognize me?"

He chuckled. "Don't be too impressed. I wouldn't have, except I saw your photograph in Friday's paper. I ran into Ruth at the grocery store and she filled me in on your taking over the business. Oh, and I keep up with Wanda and Val, too. Lots of kids, lots of fake ID's over the years."

"No need to card me now. I'm legal." I reached out to shake Shorty's hand. "And since we'll be neighbors, I figured I'd stop in and pay you a visit."

"I'm glad you did, Jackie. It's good to see people returning to Harmony. I know Ruth is happy to be out at Shady Pines with her buddies. Are you enjoying living upstairs in the old apartment?"

"Yes. I like being right on Main Street, able to see the river and all the activity here. Scott Drake remodeled it some, so it's updated now."

"The pulse of the city, right?" Shorty laughed. "This village was busy back in the day. I remember your folks. Your dad was so talented in the photography business. The missus and me still have all the photographs he took of our kids over the years. Missus hung them in the hall, and they've been there ever since. And your mother. What a beautiful woman. You look like her, you know. Maybe a bit taller."

"That's kind of you to say. I have to admit I'm surprised you're still tending bar here, Shorty."

He laughed. "Me too. Have help now, but it gives me something to keep busy with. Excuse me a second."

Shorty, who was indeed short with an ample belly, walked with a hitch and a rocking gait. He moved to serve two guys watching the game and teased them about a bet they had. I watched Shorty's reflection in the mirror above the back bar. I could see he loved being here and visiting with people. He might not know what to do with himself if not for this bar. The couple at the jukebox called out to him that they'd played one of his favorites. He nodded his thanks back at them.

How many of these small bars still exist across the

state? Another coffee-table book idea? I chuckled to myself. First the Harmony garments and then old barns. I often bit off more than I could chew.

Shorty came back, and I did what was often done here. Instead of tipping Shorty I offered to buy him a drink. "Don't mind if I do. That's mighty nice of you." He pulled a short draft of the beer I was having.

The front door opened. Shorty's expression tightened at the sight of the person walking in. I glanced in that direction. He was a young man with an angry, sullen look. He was disheveled with muddy shoes, dirty jeans, and a two-day beard growth. He looked vaguely familiar.

"The usual?" Shorty asked.

"Yeah. And give me a shot of whiskey with it," the young man said. "Been a long day."

"Working overtime again?" Shorty asked as he set down the beer and shot. Before giving an answer, the man gulped the shot.

"You might say that. Had some business to attend to out there. Moved a few things around and cleared up some paperwork with those jags." He slammed the small shot glass on the bar. "Give me another."

"Take it easy. Looks like you've had a few already."

"I have. But that's none of your business," he snarled.

"Now pour one, old man." And this time he slammed the still empty shot glass down harder.

One guy watching the game said, "Hey man, chill."

The young man got up, kicking his bar stool backwards where it crashed to the floor. He took a step toward the man. "You got a problem with me? Let's step outside."

The other guy stood, looming a good foot over him. "Maybe we should call you a ride, kid?"

"Don't bother. I'm out of here. Don't need jerks like you giving me a hard time."

"Sorry you had to see that, Jackie," Shorty said. "Kid's got issues. I feel bad for his girlfriend. I don't know why she puts up with him. She's a relative of a friend of mine, so I hear stories about him.

That's when I remembered where I'd seen the kid. He was the one who pushed past Kim and I at the construction trailer earlier.

"Does that friend happen to be Tom Lemke?"

"That's him. Nice guy. So is his great-niece. You know him?"

"I do. I met him awhile back."

"He's a lucky old coot, finally marrying the love of his life." Shorty shook his head. "Had to suffer through watching Eleanor grow up and marry four other fellas. Well, guess that last one didn't make it to the wedding.

Had to have been tough, but he just kept on working there."

"Tom and Eleanor are living in the old place now, right? I love when people name their house. What's the name for that place?"

"The Mill House," Shorty said. "I wish his great-niece would drop that bum. Tom does too. Says he treats her poorly." Shorty shrugged. "Kids though, can't tell 'em anything."

"I just met Laura today. She works at the resort sales office."

Shorty's brow furrowed, his eyes pinched with concentration. "Geez, you could be right. Last I remember, she worked at the beauty shop next to you. But I know that piece of work who just left works out there."

And he was in a furious, confrontational mood the last time I saw him, I thought. The kid seemed to drink to forget, but it wasn't working.

"Looks like he's on one hell of a bender," Shorty added. "Hate to see how booze affects some folk."

CHAPTER FIVE

Mandy and I rearranged gallery display panels because with the sales we'd made on Saturday and Sunday, we needed to fill in some empty spots.

"What a start to the new Parker Photography. And I now officially have a backlog of framing to complete," Mandy said with a wide grin. "There's an antique swap meet or market or something like that coming to town in a few weeks. I am excited to scour the booths trying to find old frames to use."

"That sounds like fun. Where are they holding it?"

"Up on the grounds of the Harmony Museum. Lots of vendors coming in. And I think there'll be some appraisers too."

"Like the Antique Roadshow?"

"Sounds like it. Say, how'd it go out at the resort construction site yesterday? Get some good ideas?" Mandy asked me.

"Kim showed me around and we met with the project's developer, Alan Morris. I'm still a bit confused about what they want and what they can afford. This might be a good job to pull you in on. You've been working the portrait part of the business and this would be a whole new area for you to learn about," I said.

"I'd love to learn how to shoot a commercial job like that. The countryside around here is so beautiful. I can't wait to see how you promote it."

"I'm just doing the photography. I'm not doing the actual promotion. But I agree that it is beautiful up in the wooded hills. Speaking of woods, what is your opinion on them taking down so many trees? I saw the protestors at the gate yesterday and that appears to be one of their issues."

"You know Jackie, I have mixed feelings about that. So many from my generation and younger aren't staying here. There just aren't enough jobs to support a family on. What they are building will bring jobs. But I know I'll miss the quiet when tourists come in. On a lighter note, I like that tourists bring more business because I have a job! And we have a brewery now too."

"Stone Mill?"

Mandy nodded.

"They are an excellent addition to Harmony," I said.

Libby jumped up on Mandy's leg for a treat she knew would be in her pocket.

"No. Sit. Stay." Mandy backed away, holding the treat in front of her. "Okay." Libby popped up and ran to her.

"You're going to have to teach me your training techniques. I'm still not good with all of that." I rubbed my little buddy's head. "But she is a sweet one. She loved chasing squirrels around in the woods and riding in the golf cart yesterday."

"Thank you again for agreeing to keep her. Matt feels bad that his allergies meant I had to give her up, but she's got the perfect new owner in you, Jackie."

"Talking about Libby reminds me of something that happened last night. I stopped by the construction trailer to get her some water and overheard a pretty intense argument. I think you might have met one of the men there. Alan Morris? He was at the party Saturday."

"That developer you mentioned before? Don't remember him."

"He arrived with Kim Walters."

"Ah yes. The tall guy with a limp? Nice dresser, I remember. But I wasn't introduced. What about him?"

"He was there with Rick Ballard, the construction

foreman who I met earlier in the day. And some guy named Winford. Do you know anyone by that name?"

"I'm sure I don't, unless he has a nickname. I mean, who uses a full first name like that? What's his last name?"

"I didn't hear it. In fact, I didn't even get to see him."

"Why are you asking?"

"I'm just a curious person, and wanted to put the argument into some context," I said.

A tapping at the front window caught our attention. It was Val, owner of the Cut-N-Curl hair salon next door. I unlocked the front door and stepped out.

"Morning Val. Opening up the salon early today?"

"Yep. Have to do that to offer a choice. In other words, someone needed an appointment and didn't call early enough so good ole Val opens up. Too bad I don't get paid overtime."

"Thanks for supporting me on Saturday," I said, giving her a hug. "It meant a lot to have my old high school buddies here with me, even if they haven't let their hair go gray yet and look ten years younger than me."

"Ten years? Seriously?" Val patted her auburn curls. "I was thinking maybe fifteen years younger. Happy Monday, my friend. Pop over for a coffee later. Wanda has an appointment to touch up her gray."

Before she unlocked the salon door, we both heard someone calling out to us. It was Stuart Walters hurrying over. He looked red-faced, obviously not used to moving so fast.

"Whoa, Stu. Slow down. You're going to give yourself a heart attack, man," Val said.

Stuart stopped in front of us, bent over, and put his hands on his knees until his heaving breaths slowed down.

"Catch your breath, Stu," I said. I ushered him to the bench I had just outside my front door.

He sat down and forced out the words. "She found a…" His chest was still heaving up and down. "…a…a body."

Stuart Walters was not used to running. This type of physical exertion was alien to him. He had a hard time catching his breath.

"Who found a body?" Val asked. "And why on earth did you run to tell us? You're not fit for that. Who is this she and was the body human or animal?"

I looked at Val over Stuart's head. I mouthed a pleading *stop it,* choking back my own laughter.

Stu looked up at me. "Kim."

"Kim found a body?"

Stu nodded.

"Okay, now tap your head twice if it was a person," Val said. "And once if it was an animal. Say, a mouse?"

With a trembling finger Stuart tapped his head. Once.

Val said. "For a dead mouse you made all this hullabaloo?"

Stu, with his finger still upside his head, just looked at us.

"Was it a spider?"

"A spider's not an animal, Val. It's an insect," I said.

We both gasped when Stu tapped his head again.

CHAPTER SIX

"**K**im called me right after she called the police," Stuart said, still struggling to calm himself. "I think she was in shock."

We soon learned that Stu had heard the news from his wife on his walk to work at the Harmony Happenings newspaper office.

"I had to find someone to help. When I saw you all out here, I came running over."

"We're glad you did, Stu," Val said. "Now fill us in."

"She had to open up the office today because Laura called in sick. First thing Kim noticed was that the office lights were left on in Winford's office. No biggie, she thinks, everyone forgets once in a while."

"So, she found Winford dead in the office?" I asked.

"No, not him. Rick Ballard is dead," Stuart said.

"Rick?" Val said. "Who's Rick?"

"The construction foreman at The Hills construction site," I told Val before looking back at Stu. "Kim found Rick dead in Winford's office?"

"No. I mean, yes. Dead, but up in the construction trailer. He was shot."

Val gasped. "Oh, my god! Who did it?"

Stuart just rocked his head slowly from side to side. "Kim has no idea. I told her I'd come right up. But Jackie, can you take me? I'm just shaking too much. And I know Kim would appreciate you being there for her."

"Of course." But not only for Kim, I thought. I'd have to tell them about my seeing Rick last night. I might have been the last person to see him alive.

As I drove, Stuart explained more of the details of what Kim discovered this morning. "Kim opened up the office because the accountant Winford didn't have his own key. The construction gate was open when she arrived, which wasn't necessarily unusual, but she noted it."

I interrupted his narrative. "I was out there last night at sunset. Rick and Alan were still there and someone else was with them. Who is this Winford you mentioned?" I asked.

"Winford Tarver is an accountant. He has a small office in with Kim at the sales building," Stuart said.

"What has Kim told you about how the units are selling? How the construction is going?"

"They are starting to sell, but there always seems to be some crisis or another. Or at least something that builds to that level. Like the protestors here on the weekends. I didn't register how many people dislike what's going on. All I heard was Kim's excitement about it. I saw how she pushed this project."

"Kim is a powerhouse, and I can understand your being swept up in her enthusiasm. What is the main issue for the protestors?"

"There are several," Stuart said. "I've done some interviews, but I'm trying to remain neutral on the issues they are raising. May I share something with you that you can't mention to Kim?"

"You know I don't like to keep secrets, Stu."

"I doubt it would ever come up in conversation with her, but I understand your hesitance. I'll just say I find it hard not to agree or at least consider some of the protestors' complaints. We'll leave it at that for now."

"I'd love to hear more about this. I just assumed it was all the new business and disruption this would bring to Harmony. Like the rock that was thrown through the Parker Photography storefront. It was never solved, but I have a good sense of who might have done it."

"Really? Who?"

"Off the record?"

Stuart Walters, the investigative reporter, chuckled before solemnly nodding. "I'm willing to pinkie swear."

"The bartender at Stone Mill Brewery, Pete. He figured out I was taking over Parker Photography, and that I was from Chicago. He didn't know it had been in my family for decades. A flash of anger crossed his eyes when he served me. That same night the rock came in."

"Seems like a big leap to me," Stuart said. "But gosh, if it's true, seems mighty petty. I don't think the protestors by the construction gate strike me as violent."

"Looks can be deceiving, Stu. I've seen protests in parts of the world that turn deadly."

"Come on, Jackie, this is Harmony, Wisconsin, not Venezuela or Hong Kong. I think most of the complaints are environmental. Folks don't like to see so many trees taken down. That causes exposed soil to become unstable. We're not getting mud slides like California, but it can get messy. One thing Kim mentioned is that they keep having to replace erosion control bags. They first thought it was a defective product, but now they are finding slits cut right in them, so any muddy slides push right on through. These protestors are cutting off their nose to spite their face. And then there are the hunters. They aren't happy about losing prime hunting lands."

As we turned in at the gate, I found myself wanting to peek at the signs I'd seen tucked away last night. What did they say? Could one protestor have gone too far? But smashing a window is a lot different from murder. Stuart was probably right. I have to scale back and remember that local people might disagree, but they wouldn't behave in a way that led to murder. More people seemed happy the project was coming than not. Or at least they accepted that things change, and this could mean a change for the better.

But the protestors might not be locals.

We pulled up at the sales office first. Stuart came hurrying back out saying that Kim was still up at the construction trailer.

We drove up to the trailer where at least six vehicles were parked, from squad cars to a coroner's van.

Kim saw us and ran over, collapsing dramatically in Stuart's arms. "This is awful. Just awful. I can't imagine finding anything like this on a Monday morning. Now I know what you felt like when you found Luella's body, Jackie. The trauma will be with me forever."

"There, there, honey. I'm here now. And aren't you glad Jackie came too?" Stuart comforted his wife.

"I am. Jackie, we're like a team. You find a body and I help you solve the crime."

I cringed at those words. Not a reputation I wanted to have.

"Except this time, I found the body. And who's always been in the mix when this happens? Alan Morris," she pronounced.

"Are you suggesting he did this?" Stuart sputtered. "Kim, don't talk nonsense."

"Oh, for god's sake Stu, that's not what I meant. It was just something I noted. He left town last night. Right Jackie? You came up here to take sunset photos, didn't you? Was Rick alive then? I know you used my golf cart because it was parked in a different spot."

Before I could answer, Chief Mathis came out of the construction trailer talking with another officer and began walking toward us.

But that didn't stop Kim from continuing. "We're trying to keep this hush-hush for now, but I'm sure many of the construction guys are hearing about it. Did you see him last night?"

"Kim honey, let's let the officers do the questioning, okay?" Stuart said.

But Kim brushed his comment off. "I'm just asking if she saw Rick last night!"

"I did. And he wasn't alone," I said.

"Well then, I think we need to talk with you, Jackie," Chief Jeff said as he came up to us.

"Of course. Kim here was just filling us in on her morning," I said.

Jeff smiled politely toward Kim. "You have been in the middle of a few interesting crimes, Kim. And now, it appears, so has Jackie. Can you stick around for a while? I'd like to ask you a few questions."

I hesitated. "Well, I rode up with Stuart..."

"I do have to get back to the paper, but I can give you some time to talk with Jeff first." Stu appeared uncertain. "You're coming back with me, aren't you Kim?"

"If Jackie stays, I stay," Kim said. "Plus, Laura isn't coming in today. I suppose we should have someone in the office."

I could tell Kim was torn. Stay and learn more about the murder. Or go back to the office to cover for Laura.

"I can give you a ride back to town, Jackie," Jeff said.

Kim reluctantly left for the sales office with Stuart, leaving me at the murder scene with the police.

Yet another murder scene, that Alan Morris was close to. Could this be a case of three strikes he's out?

CHAPTER SEVEN

I went over what happened last night with Chief Jeff. "When I arrived, there was no one at the sales office. Kim had told me to use her golf cart so off I went to explore vantage points to use for my photography. Then when I was done, I stopped by the construction trailer."

"I'm glad you came forward so quickly, Jackie," Jeff said. "Now, you stopped there why?"

"To get a little water for Libby. She'd been chasing squirrels. Plus, I wanted to sort of check in. Let Rick know I'd been here. When I got there, I saw a second car with Illinois plates, so I figured it belonged to Alan. I heard loud voices coming from inside."

Jeff pulled out a small notepad to make a couple of

notes. "Do you remember what time it was that you heard the arguing?"

"Well, I'd have to put it at just past sunset. In the hills at dusk time is hard to pinpoint. But it wasn't just the two of them. Someone else was inside too. Though he spoke little and had a soft, almost timid quality to his voice. His name was Winford. I never saw the guy, but I believe he's an onsite accountant."

"You didn't go inside the trailer?" Jeff asked.

"Correct. Libby barked, and Alan came to the door. That broke up the meeting going on inside. As I left, Alan was waiting for Winford to come out. I only saw Rick briefly when he brought a small water dish for Libby. I didn't see the third man at all. I ended up taking the golf cart back to the sales office and leaving the grounds."

Jeff asked, "Do you recall the conversation that you overheard?"

"I only heard a little bit of it. Seemed to be about money, financing, that sort of thing," I said. "Jeff, what happened? How did Rick die?"

"By gunshot, Jackie. And please keep this confidential, but we're thinking suicide," Jeff said. "We learned he kept a loaded gun in his desk drawer. Of course, we need to investigate as these things are not always clear-cut. Especially since you can place two other people here with Rick earlier in the evening. But the gun we found on the scene is registered to Rick and he was shot at close range."

"After hearing those arguments last night, I think you should consider something else, Jeff. Things got quite heated. Even threatening. Have you talked to Alan? He was very upset."

"No, we weren't aware he was even here last night until you told us just now. We'll get hold of Alan. And we're reviewing the gate security camera, which will show us who came and went late in the day. And of course, checking the gun for prints."

"I'm going back to town now with Stuart, but can I call you later?" I asked.

"Any time Jackie." Jeff said.

Stuart insisted on treating me to a maple frosted donut at Murphy's Coffee Shop when he picked some up for his office. Patti was there, and we explained to her what was happening at the resort site.

"That's hard to hear. Do they have a suspect?"

"Not that Jeff said. But they really just discovered the victim an hour ago." Of course, I kept the possible suicide idea quiet for now as Jeff had asked me to.

"And it was my sweet Kim who found the body,"

Stuart added. "What an awful way to start the week. I think I'll get a dozen donuts this morning. It's going to be a long day."

Grace Murphy boxed up Stuart's donuts while I talked more with Patti. My curiosity prompted me to ask, "Is the project up to date with fees and utilities payments?"

"I don't know current status, but since it's a matter of public record, I can tell that our treasurer has had to chase them more than once. We agreed to annex parts of the project that were outside our boundaries. So now they have to deal with us instead of the county. I can check on that for you, Jackie, and get back to you."

"Thanks, I'd appreciate that," I said.

"Is there something specific you want me to look for?" Patti asked.

"No. I'm just trying to gather a little information together. Oh, and Patti, rave reviews on your catering Saturday night!"

"Thanks Jackie, that's great to hear. It was a good opportunity for me. Excellent experience."

Stuart and I left the coffee shop. He slipped into his office and I walked back to the studio. As I passed the Cut-n-Curl, I saw Wanda settling into one of the pink salon chairs. I stuck my head in the door. "Time for a chat?"

"Hey Jackie," Val said. "Come on in and have a seat. What's the news? Was there really another murder?"

I sat on the empty chair next to Wanda and watched Val expertly touch up her gray roots. "There is a body, that's for sure. Rick Ballard, the construction supervisor."

"But why was Kim up there so early? I mean, those construction workers start at like 6:30. No way is Kim all dolled up by then," Val said.

"Stuart said that the young lady who usually opens the sales office called in sick today," I answered. "I don't think Kim got there that early. But just that she discovered the body in the construction trailer when she did," I said.

A puzzled look pinched Val's face. "Is that Laura?"

"Right, that's her," I answered.

"So, wouldn't one of the construction guys already have found Rick? Don't they coordinate and check in with him every morning?" Val wrapped Wanda's head in what looked like a shower cap. "Want some coffee, Wanda? Jackie? We've got fifteen minutes under this."

"I guess I hadn't thought of that. Good point. The call to the police came in from Kim around 9:00 this morning. I was one of the last people to see him alive last night."

"Except for the murderer," Wanda said.

"Right." Or unless it was a suicide, I thought. But Val's point was well taken. Why would Kim have been the one to make the call? Was the trailer locked?

"Well, are you going to just leave us hanging out here? Why did you see Rick last night?"

"I went out to the site at sunset to get ideas for some promotional photos. Rick was still in his office. Actually, he wasn't alone. Alan and another guy, I think maybe their accountant, were there with him. I overheard them arguing and was ready to walk away when Libby let out a yelp. So that broke up their meeting. Everyone left except Rick."

"Whoa, you seem to be right in there with another death," Wanda said. "Alan's car was gone from the Riverview this morning. Was he up at the site?"

"No. He was planning to drive back to Chicago last night."

Val sat on another chair next to us. "I'm not big on gossip, but…"

I burst out laughing and Wanda said, "Paleeze Val! Do you seriously expect us to believe that?"

Val bit her lip to keep from grinning. "What I was about to say was that Laura used to be a manicurist here. Nice kid. She also worked occasionally, on busy nights, at Shorty's Bar. She met a guy there, Tony. But he didn't like her working in the bar. Didn't like her being around a bunch of drunks, he said. She was Kim's manicurist, and Kim offered her the job at the resort's sales office when it opened up."

Wanda said, "My gossip meter hasn't reacted yet, Val. What's the rest of the story?"

"She quit Shorty's but sometimes would take appointments here on her days off, just to make extra money. I think Tony didn't like that either. The only time I met him, she and I were working on a Saturday night. He works construction somewhere I think and has to get up super early, so he lets loose on Friday and Saturday. Sounds like that's pretty normal for him. Anyway, he stumbles out of Shorty's and looks in the window. We're laughing and having a nice time, me doing Bernice's hair while Laura is doing her nails."

"Cut to the gossip, Val!" Wanda practically shouted.

"Tony comes charging in, and in a low mean voice says, *you're coming with me.* Laura can see he's been drinking. She's embarrassed and tells him she'll just quick finish up Bernice's nails. I say nothing at this point. But Bernice looks at him and says, *Can't you see we're busy here. Now go sober up.* Well, you could have heard a pin drop. Laura cowered. I mean just shrank up inside herself. She knew what was coming. Tony bends down and puts his face right up to Bernice's. I mean, like an inch apart! And he just stares at her, then reaches out and grabs Laura by the upper arm and jerks her up. Nail polish goes flying. Laura lets out an animalistic sound, like a squeal. And out they go. She hasn't worked here since then, even though customers have asked for her."

"What are you saying, Val? That Laura's calling in sick on a Monday might mean it was another terrible weekend for her and Tony?"

"I know it's nothing so serious like a murder, but Laura's in a bad spot with that boyfriend. I figured he made her quit taking the appointments here. He's half crazy. I hope Kim or someone checks in on her."

Wanda said, "Why not you, Val? Why don't you call and check on her?"

"You know you're right, Wanda. I kept my mouth closed that night. I should have stepped in then. I will, I'll call her!" Val exclaimed.

CHAPTER EIGHT

*M*andy had opened the studio doors and put out a signboard announcing our special exhibit artists. I stood back to admire it. Nice touch! Mandy's marketing abilities will be a real asset.

Libby came running out when she saw me standing on the sidewalk. "Hello there, girl." She jumped up and down against my leg. It's so nice to have someone this excited to see me. I hate to tamp down Libby's enthusiasm by making her sit first.

Mandy was watching us through the front window. She stood there shaking her head as the corners of her mouth turned up. She showed me the hand signal for sit and I bent down to give it to Libby. "Sit girl. Sit." She responded immediately. Mandy gave me a thumbs up before she walked away from the window.

I squatted down next to Libby and gave her a hug. "Good girl. You're being very patient with me."

"She wants to please you, Jackie and make you happy," Scott said as he appeared unexpectedly by my side.

I stood up and smiled. "Scott! Nice to see you. I'm realizing that. I'm so happy Libby came into my life."

"Lots of us here in Harmony want to make you happy, you know."

He reached out his hand to help me, which I appreciated as I sometimes forget how difficult it is getting for me to stand back up. My thigh strength isn't what it used to be. I need to get some power walking in. Maybe bicycling, too.

He continued speaking. "My daughter-in-law Mandy scolded me for missing your grand opening. She let me know what a great success it was. I came over to check out the new place and offer my apologies for not being here Saturday night. Sounds like I missed a good party."

"That's okay, Scott. I understand you were enjoying a fishing trip to Minnesota. Did Mandy show you what we did with the place?"

"You pulled everything together beautifully. This is the first time I've seen it all fancied up since the remodeling. Great touches you've added. This will be an enormous asset to our Main Street."

I was glad Scott stopped by. "You missed seeing your son trying out a new career."

"I heard Patti kept him busy!" Scott said.

"I've done some decorating upstairs. Would you like to see that?"

"I can't right now. Work awaits. But I'd like to make plans to see it soon. Can I call you?"

"Of course," I said. Then quickly added, "I look forward to it."

"Me too, Jackie."

I watched him walk away toward his pickup truck parked down the street. Sounds of giggling brought me back to the moment at hand. Embarrassed, I turned to see Aunt Ruth and her Shady Pines gals wiggling their shoulders, winking, and sending air kisses.

"Ha ha. How long have you been standing there?" I asked.

"Long enough," Ruth said. "Now if I can manage to pull you away from watching that hunk of manhood, I'd like to show the gals the changes you made to my old apartment."

"Sure, come on, I'll show you around."

After the tour of the second story remodeling, the gals invited me to join them for drinks at Shady Pines later. "Tell you what, I was planning on hiking the Go

Around walking path later. It goes right past Shady Pines, doesn't it?"

"Yes, it does," Eunice said. "We've walked sections of it ourselves. I don't think the entire thing is paved yet, though. Supposed to be, but that's government for you."

"I plan on forging on through whatever lies in those, what is it, five or six miles?" I said.

"Don't mind her, Jackie. It might not be paved, but the trail bed is laid for the entire route. My daughter has taken her grandchildren on it numerous times," Dorothy said.

Betty said, "Five miles? All in one evening. I think I'd have to take a tent and camp halfway around."

I put my arm around her shoulder. "I'll pack supplies, but I think I'll be okay, Betty. You can light a candle and I'll watch for your signal. A cold beer might be appreciated too."

"Or a glass of wine?" Betty said.

"I'll take whatever you offer! See you all later."

"And then you can tell us what they found out about that murder at The Hills," Ruth said. "We have only heard bits and pieces. Like that the police already interviewed you."

"Now, how did you know that?" I asked. "Never mind, I will eventually remember that news travels quick around here."

The gals had just left when Hannah, from Sutton's Antiques, crossed the street. She exchanged a few words with Aunt Ruth before stepping inside the gallery.

"Congratulations Jackie, the grand opening was a success! Mark and I had a lovely evening."

"I appreciate that Hannah, and I feel properly welcomed back to Harmony!"

"And ready to tackle that garments through the decades project at the museum? I'm super excited about it. I'm hoarding antique dress forms to display the pieces. We're having good luck finding many of the garments in original Harmony family portraits Eleanor has shared with us. We are pinning down dates they were worn more accurately, especially with help from the Shady Pines gals," Hannah said. "They've spent hours poring over photos and papers."

"I'm looking forward to it as well. Do you have other help from the Historical Society too?"

"I do. There are three other women working on this with me. I believe you met one of them, Kay Whitlow, at that meeting after the fundraising gala. Anyway, you'll meet them all, eventually. Does Thursday work for you?"

I turned to Mandy. "Okay with you, Mandy? I want you to be part of this project. It'll be wonderful to learn about lighting for commercial photography."

"I'm good with that," Mandy said. "I'll ask Ruth to run the shop for a few hours."

"An apprentice?" Hannah said.

Mandy replied, "Jackie's teaching me about outdoor photography too. Up at The Hills building site. Say, Mrs. Sutton, did you hear about the murder there this morning?"

"What? Another murder? No, I didn't. Who was it?"

"The construction foreman, Rick Ballard. Kim Walters found him," Mandy said.

"Do they know who did it?" Hannah asked.

"Not yet," I said. "And we don't know if it's a murder for sure. Very tragic. Did you know him?"

"Don't recognize the name. He might have been from out of town. Many of the guys working there are. They're putting them up at the motel out by the freeway entrance."

"But some are local?" I asked.

Mandy said, "Matt told me that Bill Collins, Tony Keaton, Craig Ramirez, and Lucas Bailey are working there. In fact, it's cutting into some projects him and his dad are doing. But he says he doesn't blame them. The money is good."

Then it is true that Laura's boyfriend Tony works at The Hills. Maybe he wanted to be able to keep an eye on her.

CHAPTER NINE

The map of Mary's Go Around Trail came out of my printer. I had uploaded it in my phone too, but better safe than sorry since I sometimes lose my cellular signal in these hills. Another thing to add to my transition list…check on getting a different cellphone carrier. Ah, but now, a peaceful nature hike with my little buddy Libby.

The trail started out years ago as just a path along the edge of the Wisconsin River flowing through town. Other trails, like the one that left from behind the Riverview Motel, were connected over the years. Now it reached the point of a complete six-mile loop, expanding to over ten miles, depending on which side trails you took.

Thank you, Mary, whoever you were!

I packed a sandwich and water bottle in my backpack. I walked north up the hill from Main Street, through residential areas, including Oak Street, where my family home was.

From there I could catch the Go Round above town. Then east through the hilly forests, dipping back down to the river near Shady Pines. I should make it to the gals' Happy Hour by the looks of it.

After that, I'd take the path west along the river and pass by the Stone Mill Brewery on its backside. The downtown waterfront parks and stores would be next. By that time, if Libby was too tired, I could drop her at home while I continued on west to the marina where I'd check to see if Rocco Montalvo was in town. I hadn't seen him since I'd moved back. From there the loop trail left the river and headed up behind the Riverview Motel.

According to the map, the trail passed near the Harmony House Museum and Nature Center. I'm sure there would be side trails there. I made tentative plans to enjoy my sandwich at a picnic table on the grounds. Then I'd reconnect with the main trail and end up back on the north side of Harmony to catch the trailhead where I'd started. Ending with an easy downhill walk to Main Street.

With my Happy Hour stop at Shady Pines, and my

sandwich picnic stop, I should be gone well over two hours, maybe three, depending on Libby's walking speed.

Over my years of visiting Harmony, I'd rarely walked up to Oak Street, my old neighborhood. There was a part of me that didn't want to see it I suppose. Way too many memories best left in the past. The photography studio filled me with happy memories, and I embraced those.

As I crossed Oak Street, the sounds and smells of the afternoon took me back to growing up here. The fresh cut grass smells never grew old. Definitely something I missed living in downtown Chicago. Backyard swings squeaked as children pumped their legs higher and higher. Dogs barked at nothing and everything.

I knew that the B&B Todd was staying at was down this street a couple of blocks. But the trail called me. I imagined at this hour Todd was still enjoying the Frank Lloyd home, studios, and grounds anyway.

Plus, I realized how much I was looking forward to taking this walk with Libby and just my thoughts. I might check in with Todd though when I came back this way later.

I found a trail arrow pointing toward a moss-covered stone arch. Why was the entrance here? This didn't look like a trailhead. Shortly after I entered under the arch, I realized I was in a cemetery. A very old one, with signs asking for respectful silence for the souls resting here. Obviously intended for those of us passing through to get to the trail. Was this an old family cemetery? Some of the headstones no longer stood properly upright. A monolith contained names of those buried here, whose headstones were now illegible or buried under the topsoil. If I intended to finish the loop before dark, I'd better keep going. Reading names of dead people I didn't know was not part of my plan.

The cemetery path soon joined up with a paved portion of the Go Round Trail. A map carved into the surface of a simple wooden podium showed me a *You Are Here* sign with a red dot. I made a right, heading in a northeasterly direction. Soon the path had me walking out in the country, far above Main Street.

As the elevation leveled out, Libby and I both found a comfortable strolling pace. I unleashed her, knowing she was a good dog and would stay near me. Occasional flat lands were fenced for grazing cattle. I caught peeks of barns and houses, then back into the shadows of maples and oaks. Tall sturdy pines mixed in among the deciduous species still pushing out their summer foliage.

Always carry a camera was my motto, and its strap hung around my neck now. Libby walked in the forest parallel to me, sniffing for whatever it is dogs sniff for, when her body went into alert mode. I called her name just as she made a bolt after a squirrel.

Sun beams cut through the forest at a sharp angle, creating an eerie and unreal fairy-like landscape. I pulled out my camera. Zooming in and out I caught sight of the weathered gray surface of a building. I didn't want to be caught photographing someone's backyard, but on closer examination through my lens, the building appeared to be unused. My natural curiosity got the best of me and I stepped off the trail and into the forest.

Libby joined me just as I got to the other side of the narrow strip of forest. The tree line ended. Nestled in among the hills was a small abandoned farm.

Total silence.

Lifeless buildings.

Time stopped here.

I've wanted to do a coffee-table photograph book about the left behind farms. The ones that have stopped being family supporting operations. The ones with the sadness cloaking them. The ones once full of life and growth, now quietly fading into oblivion. I want to capture them with my photography. This one, which serendipitously came to me, might be a perfect start.

The outbuildings in my line of vision were not yet collapsing. They tempted me to venture further, but I knew hours could go by if I began exploring. I zoomed in on one of the house windows where curtains hung limply, blurring the interior. Yes, this speaks to me. I'll research the family who lived here and try to fill out parts of their life through the rare photos of them that might still exist. The idea to do overlays of my photographs and those from the past popped into my head. That technique would work well with this project.

Time stood still here.

But now Robert Frost's poem about miles to go before I sleep whispered in my ears.

At least I wasn't on a snowy path, I was enjoying a sunny day. But it did give me the push required to move on. This place would be here in the future. And I had a happy hour waiting for me on the path ahead.

I felt compelled to look back at the farm and whisper, I'll be back. I called to Libby, and we made our way back to the trail.

CHAPTER TEN

The downhill trail back toward the river was steep. No one else was out today. I suppose Monday evenings were for relaxing after a weekend of outdoor activity. The trail crossed the main road into Harmony and led me back to the river's shoreline east of town.

The gals waited on benches resting on the pine needle floors just up from the river. They'd set up drinks and snacks on trays. I quickly called Libby back from racing up to snag one of the little sausages or the ham-wrapped pickles. But Ruth covered for me as she bent over and scooped Libby up to hold in her lap. Hugs and kisses followed with Libby's entire body wiggling round and round, up and down.

"We're having an hors d'oeuvres dinner," Betty exclaimed. "Isn't this just perfect?"

It was perfect. Aunt Ruth looked so happy here. Her friendships with these women were priceless. Now life brought them together once again.

"How was your walk so far?" Eunice asked. "We can drive you home if you're too tired to keep going."

"I'm good, but I think I may drop Libby off at the apartment. That's about the halfway point and until I get her used to walking longer distances, I don't want to wear her out," I said.

Eunice handed me an ice-cold beer. "We put our minds together and thought this was the best drink for you. Cold and refreshing."

At the same time Dorothy put a small bowl of water down for Libby.

"Thank you and cheers," I said, raising my bottle in a toast. "Here's to many more hikes past Shady Pines."

"Now share with us what you know about that awful event this morning," Aunt Ruth demanded. "I promised the girls you'd have some news."

"Sorry to disappoint, but I'm not really involved in this one. Kim found the body of the construction foreman, Rick Ballard this morning. Chief Jeff questioned me because I'd seen Rick last night. I was scouting locations for publicity photographs and had just seen him."

"I swear that place is jinxed. Haunted. First Paul Griffin's death. Wasn't he involved in some way with it?" Betty asked.

"Kind of, in a sort of indirect way," I said.

"And then Luella Hagge's murder!" Ruth exclaimed. "I heard she was doing some underhanded dealings with permits and stuff."

"Oh yes, conspiracies abound, swirling all crazy-like across those hills," Eunice said. "If it was up to all the nosy ones, a spacecraft would have landed on the construction site and zapped protestors away into space."

Betty's eyes flew wide open. "I hadn't thought of that!"

"The point my friend Eunice is trying to make is that until they solve the case," Dorothy said, "We count on you, Jackie, to keep us from making stuff up."

I joined the laughter. "I will. Now you all stop spreading rumors about hovering spacecraft and I will find out about the investigation for you. How's that sound?"

"Like a reasonable solution," Dorothy said. "I think we should all just chill. The murder just happened this morning."

"Well, it appeared he died last night," I said.

"So see, it's almost twenty-four hours old. What's

that TV show about solving a crime in twenty-four hours. They better get going," Betty said.

"Betty, don't get all worked up. It's called *48 Hours*," Eunice mumbled.

"Well good, then we have some time left," Betty said with a loud sigh.

With an amused smile Dorothy said, "You'd better get moving, Jackie. Don't want to get caught out in the dark."

Finishing up my beer, I leashed up Libby. She'd had a rest and was ready to go on with our grand adventure. I waved goodbye and headed west.

There was a quiet stretch on the trail before hitting the old industrial side of Harmony. The rehabbed paper mill appeared. The beauty and strength of the building was obvious from this approach. A few boats were docked at the public pier. The old dock sat slightly above the river and the trail rose above it, walking right at the edge of the Stone Mill Brewery's outdoor patio. I didn't recognize anyone seated outside, but I received and returned friendly waves. My thoughts went to the night when I'd been threatened here. It was under construction then, closed to customers. Seemed like a long time ago.

The trail sloped down to shoreline level again as I

continued toward the downtown area. Ahead, I saw the village commons.

"Well girl, this is the last chance to stop your part of the journey." Libby looked rested after our visit at Shady Pines, but I took a couple minutes to drop her back at the apartment before I continued on and finished the loop. Libby was obviously ready to stay home. She quickly settled in her doggie bed near the glass door of the balcony.

Now returning to the trail, the walk along the river stretched ahead of me. I was good with time. I knew I didn't want to be caught in the dark hills after the sun sank behind them. Even after dark, it would feel safe compared to living in a big city where your antenna had to be out. I should get some light reflective gear and maybe one of those headlamps. And a bike! Perfect path for a bike. It would take some training for me to peddle up the hills here, but it was something to look forward to.

Right now my focus was on finding Rocco Montalvo's boat at the marina up ahead. Most of the slips were taken. The place seemed to be thriving.

I waved to Travis Harris, Val's son, who I learned was now in charge of the Lake Harmony marina and boat slips. The so-called lake was really just a very wide part of the river, controlled by a dam. It was part of the Wisconsin River, but we claimed it as our lake.

"Hey Ms. Parker, how's it going?" Travis insisted on formally addressing me long after he'd grown up. "Heard you're moved into the old apartment. Welcome home. I know Mom is glad to have you back."

"She told me you were running this place. How is your wife? I can't wait to meet your little ones one of these days."

"Marissa's fine. Busy with the twins and all their activities. We're making plans to expand the marina once summer is over."

"In anticipation of all the tourists moving into the new development?" I asked.

"Right," Travis said. "Bought some property further east, upriver, where we can have dry dock space for repairs and cleaning. Plus, now we will have more room to store boats over winter too."

"Is that near the Stone Mill Brewery? I just walked by there and saw a sign that read *Future Home of Harris & Sons.*"

Travis gave me a sheepish grin. "I thought the name sounded great. The boys are in their teens and are both already helping out here. Does it sound like I'm expecting too much?"

"Not at all, Travis! Wish you much success with the

business. I'm glad to see that area being put to use again. Is there a Rocco Montalvo docked here? He's from Chicago, but I think he's staying on his boat here now."

Travis showed me the way to Rocco's boat. What would have been a midsize cruiser in one of Chicago's lakefront harbors on Lake Michigan looked like a yacht here.

"Hey Mr. Montalvo, you've got a visitor," Travis called out. Rocco's head appeared at the railing of the flying bridge above me.

"Permission to board," I called up to him.

"Jacqueline! Of course, come on board."

"Good to see you again," Travis said. "I'll be getting back to work."

I used the boat ladder to climb onboard the *Roccome Baby.*

"Jacqueline, this is such a great surprise."

"I'm happy to find you here. I didn't know how often you came into town," I said. "What a beautiful cruiser. But is the name Rocco Me? Or more like saying welcome with an accent?"

"Whatever way you want to read it I'm fine with. It came from my wife's love of jazz. One of her favorites was B.B. King doing Rock Me Baby. She performed in local jazz clubs and she'd sing right to me...*rock me baby, rock me all night long.* Now this lady rocks me all night long so to speak," Rocco said with a wink. "But enough of that, let me show you around my *Roccome Baby*."

I took in all the details of the finely crafted boat. It was a beauty. The wood gleamed. The deck was spotless.

"To what do I owe this pleasure?" Rocco asked.

"I was in the neighborhood walking the Go Round Trail. But do I need a reason?"

Rocco laughed. "Of course not my dear, but I strongly suspect you have one."

He had me there.

"Well, there is the death that happened last night." I told him what I knew, including what I heard last night.

"And they are calling it a suicide. Am I right?" Rocco asked. "Wait, I know you can't answer that. I imagine Chief of Police Mathis, if he told you that, would have also requested you not mention it to anyone. But the look on your face gave it away. I know you have a couple miles walking ahead of you and you want to keep the daylight. So, much as it hurts me, I will relinquish the pleasure of your company to assure the daylight illuminates your way along the trail. But can we meet for breakfast at the Harmony Diner, finest breakfast establishment between here and Chicago? I would like to check on a few things."

"With your people back in Chicago?" I asked, knowing Rocco was a private investigator working for an investment group that was funding The Hills. Perfect, I thought. I'd get another perspective on what was going on.

He nodded. "Now off with you, so this old man can make some phone calls."

I left the harbor and continued along the river. When the Riverview Motel appeared, the trail wound past it and up the hill. Memories of my discovery of Paul Griffin's car accident flooded over me. Wanda and I had been hiking and discovered the body on the morning of what was to be his wedding day to Eleanor Harmony. Finding love in your eighties is unusual in itself, but Eleanor did it twice that year.

Paul had been involved with Alan Morris in putting together the original resort and golf course deal. Even before the accident, Paul pulled out of the deal. Alan was still part of it. By the scene at the construction trailer last night, in up to his eyeballs.

I saw signs on the path pointing the way toward the Harmony House Museum and Nature Center, but I opted out of going there tonight. The journey was taking longer than I expected so I just sat on a bench looking out over treetops to distant hills. The bench was dedicated to Constance Harmony. Eleanor must have donated it in honor of her mother. Her recent donation of the mansion and grounds to the Historical Society meant the history of Harmony would have a home for generations to come.

I pushed myself up and stretched. The last leg of my journey was ahead. Soon enough I arrived back at the path that entered the graveyard. I came out under the stone arch, putting me back into my old neighborhood.

The sun was setting. Oak Street was lined with classic styled streetlamps. Their dim glow lighting my way. The Whitlow Bed and Breakfast caught my eye even from a distance. Most of this area's homes were well maintained and stylishly landscaped and decorated, but nothing like the Whitlow B&B. Candles were lit in every window. Up lighting for the gigantic oaks heightened their majesty. Fairy lights twinkled in several large shrubs near the porch. Lit lamps shone on the tables of the sprawling front porch.

As I approached the B&B, Todd came around the corner. "Hi JP. What a pleasant surprise. I was hoping to see you once more and say thank you for inviting me to your gallery opening. It brought me to your charming little hometown."

"You're welcome, Todd. How was your day at Taliesen?"

"Amazing! And I just grabbed a burger at this place

on the river before walking back here. Love the Lake Michigan shoreline, but this river setting is stunning. I'm already booking a room for the fourth of July and plan on bringing a couple of friends."

"I'm so happy to hear that!"

"Believe me Jackie, your studio will get a glowing write up. I'm loving that I booked my room here because it makes me feel like a local. Kay has put up such history of the city with all the photos she has on her walls. It's like everyone knows everyone. You're all connected. She mentioned that your family had a home near here. I thought you grew up in the apartment above the studio."

"Most of my fondest memories of my childhood were from that apartment. But yes, my family had a home here. Want to take a little walk further and I'll show you my old place? I haven't gone by it in years and I'd like to see how she's looking."

I hooked arms with Todd as we walked west along Oak Street. I was glad he was with me and would give me support.

The house looked remarkably like it had fifty years ago. Some landscaping was changed. Shrubs had outgrown their life and were replaced. But even the new ones had the same symmetry and order as when my family lived here. Low bushes framed the front steps.

Potted plants sat on each stair tread, just like we'd done it.

"Getting nostalgic, JP?" Todd asked.

I did some quick blinking to clear the tears I felt forming. "Sure am." I squeezed his arm. "Thank you for checking it out with me. She looks as grand as ever."

The shadow of someone moved in what used to be my bedroom window. Two young children played on the front porch. Their grandmother rocked in a white wicker rocker, watching them. She looked up and waved at Todd and me.

"Everybody waves. I love it! It's remarkable how well maintained these places are. Like Kay's, too. She has done a terrific job with the place. I enjoyed meeting the other guests there as well. Very homey," Todd said.

I turned to walk Todd back to his place. "I'm ready to call it a night. Safe travels back to Chicago tomorrow."

"I think I'll grab a wine and sit out on the porch a bit. Soak up the quiet life before going back to the chaos. There's another guest from Chicago. He's doing some sort of work here and won't leave for a few more days."

"That's nice."

"I've tried to get him to chat, but he's kind of timid and a little peculiar, fussy, maybe is the word. Always leaves his shoes by the back door. Who does that in a hotel?"

CHAPTER ELEVEN

A hot morning shower helped my aching legs. That was a long walk yesterday. But no regrets. It felt wonderful. After my morning cup of coffee, I was ready to welcome the day. Earlier I took Libby out to the small private outdoor space Scott had created behind the studio. It had been unused for years. Scott enclosed the back staircase and built a garage creating a little patch of green yard. Perfect for Libby in the morning!

I'd hit the hay as soon as I got home last night, barely making it into my pajamas after washing my face. And I dreamed of my childhood. I'm sure seeing the house last night had prompted the dreams. Only snippets remained for me this morning…long dark hallways… closed doors…a frantic feeling. Empty suitcases, that I was supposed to pack, but I didn't know with what. Urgent whispers elsewhere in the house. I couldn't find anyone to ask what I should pack. I was alone.

Not a pleasant dream, but it was what it was and now I was wide awake, ready to meet Rocco at the diner.

My cell rang with a phone call from Kim. I hoped she'd have more information to share with me.

"Good morning, Kim. How are you doing?"

"Great. I hoped you and I might touch base. Keep each other in the investigative loop, so to speak."

Kim's tone of voice suggested she knew something.

"That's thoughtful of you to think about me," I said. "But you really should tell Chief Jeff if you have pertinent information."

"Oh, I did. That's how I learned they thought it was a suicide. But…" A long pause followed. I almost hung up thinking the call had dropped. "…it could have been a murder!"

"Oh, really? What makes you think that?"

"Jeff didn't tell me directly, but rumors are flying around the site. Like why was Rick there so late on a Sunday? Was he meeting someone who did him harm and made it look like suicide? Money troubles came up repeatedly. Even, and this is no way concrete, just gossip at this point. I'm sure you'll take it with a grain of salt, but there is speculation about drugs moving in and out of the site."

"Sounds like most of this is just workplace gossip as you put it Kim. So yes, I'll take it for gossip, but I won't rule out that there could be grains of truth in it. And that's what should be investigated."

"I know the money angle is real. We've had issues with that all along during this process. Checks to the village clerk have bounced and had to be reissued. I get complaints from employees about their paychecks, and vendors who stop here with unpaid invoices. I can't help them. It's not part of my job."

"Are you sure they can afford my fees for the promotion?" I asked.

"Ooh, good point, Jackie. Let me check further on that. The investors sent that Winford guy to check things out, so they must have suspicions too. Just like me!"

"Maybe Rick committed suicide over money troubles? Or maybe he thought he was close to getting caught doing something fraudulent? Are they focusing on that?" I asked.

"Exactly. Wait, no. Not exactly. I was thinking maybe Rick caught someone else embezzling. But when you say that, I have to rethink it. He could have been. Oh gosh, Jackie. This makes my head hurt. I thought Alan did it, that he killed Rick. You heard them arguing, after all. And I hear Alan complain about money. He said the investors are coming into Harmony this weekend. The pressure is mounting. And maybe he just snapped!"

"Who snapped? Rick or Alan?" I asked. She even had me confused.

"Both? Either one? Darn, here I thought I had it figured out. Now I can't even remember which thing made the most sense. Rick killed himself because he was going to be caught cheating, cooking the books. Or Alan killed him because he knew what Alan was doing and would turn him in." Then in one of those catch her breath but keep going moments she added, "Ooh, another idea just came to me. Alan killed him because they are in it together. Joint fraud. And Alan didn't want Rick to get his share of the money."

"Boy, oh boy Kim. You are really looking at this from all angles."

Remembering Val's comments about Laura, and Mandy telling me about Tony working at the site, I decided Kim might be just the person to ask how that situation was going.

"Thanks, Jackie. I feel like my mind just keeps coming up with stuff like that. It's a blessing and a curse I suppose."

I was glad we were on the phone and Kim couldn't

see my facial expressions. I wanted to redirect her focus. "Kim, was Laura feeling better and able to come in today?"

"Yes, she was. Poor thing. She was just crushed when she heard about Rick. I mean, we all were, but she took it extra hard for some reason. I was thinking she maybe had a concussion. She didn't go into the doctor to check out that possibility. Oh no. Even today I could see she had bruising from the fall she claimed happened. Supposedly that's why she didn't come in on Monday."

My antenna popped up with that information. So, Laura claimed she fell, and that's why she didn't come in.

"Oh dear. I hope she's alright. This all has to be such a shock for those of you who worked for him. Didn't Laura's boyfriend work construction for Rick?"

My question opened the floodgates.

"Confidentially Jackie, her boyfriend is a jerk. I don't think she fell. I think he hit her. And this isn't the first time. He's such a jealous person. And for no reason. Tony, that's the boyfriend's name, hated Rick because he thought he was flirting with Laura. But keep this between us, I don't want to get Laura involved. Tony will beat her up again if he thinks she's talking to me about their relationship."

"Goodness. Someone needs to talk to Laura. To help

her out of a bad situation if that's true. Do you think Rick was attracted to Laura?" I asked.

"Laura claims not. He was acting as more of a big brother. He sensed the meanness in Tony and tried to talk Laura into leaving him. But not for Rick, you understand. Just for her own good. My head is spinning! All these tangled story lines. It's just all too much, Jackie!"

"Kim, I think this is something you should talk to Jeff about. He can interview Tony without involving Laura. But Laura herself might be in danger if Tony is as you describe him."

"Really? You think so? I know Tony is a nasty person. I don't want to make things worse for Laura. Or for me. He came to me complaining about getting his check late. Me. Why me? I'm a realtor, not head of payroll depart-ment." And she spun on a dime to say, "Can you come out here Wednesday? I've hired a drone flier to take some images. Have you ever done that? It's perfect for this type of place, isn't it?"

I am sometimes left breathless at how suddenly Kim's conversation and attention switch up. So, I didn't ask any further questions but simply said. "I'm late for a breakfast meeting. But yes, I'd love to see the drone operate. I'll see you Wednesday morning."

After hanging up with Kim, my mind was still spinning. I don't know how Stuart keeps up with her. Once my head cleared after our meandering conversation, I knew I'd be left with some things to think about.

As soon as I got to the diner, I learned Rocco had thoughts about Rick's death too. By the time Dolly put his coffee down, he was already filling me in on what he'd learned.

"I spoke with several people after you left last night. Alan didn't answer my calls, which is curious. But then with the way things have been going, he rarely has good news for me."

"What things?" I asked, remembering how he'd been arguing with Rick on Sunday night.

"It's a mix of stuff. Between the construction foreman and the onsite accountant, Alan is being pinched. And the rumor mill is indicating the police are fully investigating it, though at first it appeared to have been a suicide."

"Is the accountant's name Winford by any chance?" I asked.

"It is, how did you know that?"

I explained about my being at the site on Sunday and overhearing the arguing.

"Interesting," Rocco remarked. "A few questionable irregularities caught their eye last month, and my investors were insistent on bringing their own guy in to manage the books. They'd worked with Winford Tarver before. In fact, they are planning on coming this weekend to go over things with Alan and Rick. Obviously Rick will no longer be part of that conversation. Tarver is not only running the financials, but has been auditing the books prior to his arrival on the scene. He's found some interesting things for them to look over. Apparently, he's keeping them in the loop. Thus, the meeting this weekend. Alan Morris is going to be called up on the carpet for all the financial irregularities discovered. And even if it doesn't involve him, and only involved Rick, it still has been happening on his watch."

"What do you think happened to Rick?"

"I'm not ruling suicide out. He could have had personal things in his life that were too much to handle. Things we don't know about. I know that the police will investigate that. But I learned there was no suicide note. If we uncover Rick's involvement being deeper than we thought, it could be a reason to commit suicide. But also a reason to be taken out... murdered. I'm thinking that Alan might have been working with Rick."

"I can see how that could happen. And Alan is lying low, which speaks to him being guilty too."

"They probably have a ballistic report, but I imagine it will show the bullet came from Rick's own handgun. I've already checked, and Alan carries a FOID card. It would have been easy enough for Alan to make it look like a suicide."

I knew what he meant. I had a FOID card myself. Firearm Owners Identification card is a requirement to own guns in Illinois. "So, you're actually thinking Alan may have done it?"

"It's a strong possibility in my mind."

"You may not know this, but two other times Alan has been at the edges of murders here in Harmony."

Rocco took a sip of his coffee, set the cup down and said, "This might be a case of three strikes you're out."

"My thought exactly."

CHAPTER TWELVE

*T*hurried to the Cut-n-Curl for a hair appointment with Val. "Sorry if I'm a little late. It's been a long morning."

"No problem, Jackie. I'm excited to have my hands in your hair again. When was the last time?" Val said.

"I think the sleepover at Wanda's house when we were commiserating over boyfriends…"

"Or lack thereof?"

"Right. We all picked a career that night. No waiting for husbands. We'd forge our own path in the world. I was going to be a photographer. You wanted to own a hair salon. And Wanda? What was her thing?"

Val laughed as she wrapped me in her pink shampoo cape. "Wanda's plan was to marry John. She couldn't see any further than that. God, she was goo-goo eyed over him. You want the same basic style, just a trim?"

"Just a trim. And not like you gave me that night of the sleepover. You assured me that the pile of hair laying on Wanda's bathroom floor just looked big. That you really hadn't cut off too much. You practically shaved my head!"

"I was going for the Mia Farrow look," Val said indignantly. "It was all the rage. In fact, I think with your bone structure you'd look…" She snipped her scissors opened and closed, coming closer and closer to my hair.

"Don't you dare!"

The front door jingled.

"Hey there Kay, you're a little early. I'm not quite finished here. I've got the new People magazine in. Have a seat."

I looked in the mirror in front of me. It was Kay Whitlow, the woman I met at the Historical Society meeting.

She spoke first. "Aren't you Jacqueline Parker? I think we met a few months ago. I'm Kay Whitlow."

"Yes, I remember you. Nice to see you again. But please, call me Jackie."

Kay sat down in the waiting chairs and said, "Love your gray hair, Jackie. I hope mine looks as nice as that when the time comes."

"Thanks Kay, I love not covering the gray roots anymore. Wanted to let you know I have a friend, Todd Baldwin, staying at your B&B and he loves it," I said.

"He is such a sweet guy. So interested in Harmony. He told me he was in town to report on your opening gala for a Chicago publication."

"Yes," I said. "He's a marketing guru."

"I attended, but I didn't get to say hello to you. It was a lovely event. Your gallery and studio will be a wonderful addition to Main Street. Hopefully, the big resort project going on up in the hills will bring in the tourists and we'll continue to grow as a must-see tourist destination."

"Thank you, Kay. Todd mentioned all the photographs you have displayed at the house. He said there was one of a family in front of the studio. The way he described it I think that might have been me with my mother and father. I'd love to stop up and see it sometime if that's okay."

"Of course," Kay said. "I'd love to show you. Hannah and I are working on duplicating some of mine for display at the Harmony House. And I'm excited to be working with you on the garment project as well."

Val explained to Kay that Hannah's antique shop used to be my mother's dress shop. "So it's a perfect circle of life sort of moment that Jackie is working with fancy dresses now too, don't you think?"

"That is a delightful story," Kay said. "I know which photograph you mean. I thought of using it to do a sort of time lapse Tim Burton sort of video. A photo compilation of Main Street now and then."

I took note that Kay and I thought alike. That is the type of thing I wanted to do with the old farms I planned on photographing.

Val said, "That sounds cool! You all are so creative. Kay's B&B has been written up in some travel magazines. Each bedroom is loaded with antiques."

"How many bedrooms do you have?"

"There are six. Each has a bath which involved substantial remodeling, but much as today's traveler wants to stay at a historic home, they don't want to live with historic plumbing arrangements," Kay said with a chuckle. "Scott Drake helped me straighten everything out in a creative and affordable manner. One doesn't go into the bed-and-breakfast industry to build a big retirement nest egg."

"Nor into hairdressing," Val said. "Do you have a good occupancy rate?"

"Seasonal like many businesses around here. We do good during the fall colors and of course over the

Christmas holidays. Harmony really turns on the charm then. Then we go into our slow season. Valentine's Day books up, and some at Easter for families coming into town to visit relatives. I promote with a newsletter trying to bring in groups, like women get-togethers. Summer is the busiest, of course. Right now, I have four rooms filled, which for a Tuesday this early in the season is good. Oh wait, make that three, your friend Todd left this morning. And I have one guy who's booked for almost three weeks, which is unusually long. The other two rooms are returning guests, two couples who drive across country to their summer homes in Montana."

"I'll look forward to seeing the house."

"And I'd love to do some cross promoting if that's alright. I'll put your business up in my newsletter and maybe you can display some of your work in my house?" Kay said.

"Sounds like a good idea."

"There you go, Jackie. All done!" Val said.

My curiosity about what was going on with Rick Ballard's investigation got the better of me. I decided I'd just casually stroll by the police station, but of course it was very much on purpose. But Jeff wasn't in. I called him and left a message.

Now what to do for supper. Hmm, maybe take my little buddy out to the marina where they have that hot dog stand. A good Chicago style hot dog would taste great. Libby was certainly up for it.

I'd already gotten to the Go Round by the river when Jeff returned my call. "Hi Jackie, are you up for a burger and beer at the Stone Mill? I could meet you there in half an hour. Want to ask your opinion about something."

"I'd love to, Jeff. Do they allow dogs on the patio? I'm out for a walk with Libby."

"I think they do."

"Then I'll meet you there," I said, wondering what he wanted my opinion on.

Benny Spencer, the manager at Stone Mill Brewery, greeted me at the door. "Jackie, how nice to see you again." He looked down at Libby. "Patio okay? We don't allow dogs inside."

"Yes, it is. And put me in the sun please, it's cooling off and old ladies get cold easily."

"Nonsense, you can't be over forty!"

"Hilarious," I said with an eye roll. "And a table for two."

"We have heat lamps out there as well. You just let me know and I can turn it on for you."

Benny led me to a nice sunny spot. I ordered the Pulp Man Red Ale, appropriately named as this had been a paper mill at one time.

I sat next to the railing separating the patio from the Go Round trail I walked last night. I enjoyed people watching while I waited for Jeff. A small speed boat tied up at the dock. A young couple walked the concrete steps up to the patio. Hikers pushing baby strollers passed. Because the path narrowed here, cyclists walked their bikes through this section.

Jeff approached the patio from the side path along the edge of the building, surprising me by covering my eyes with his hands.

"Guess who?"

"The handsomest police man east of the Mississippi and north of the Wisconsin River?"

"No, it's me, Jeff."

I laughed out loud and stood up to give him a hug. He'd changed into civilian clothes, his slightly longer than regulation hair just touching the collar of his denim shirt.

"You look as good as always, Jackie. Thanks for agreeing to meet me here. And hey there Libby," Jeff said ruffling his hands through her hair.

Our waiter took our orders of hamburgers, and Jeff ordered the same beer I was having.

"Now what was it you wanted my advice on, Jeff?"

"This is awkward, but I wanted to ask your advice on dating."

My heart started a quick little pitter patter. And my breath caught in my throat.

"You see, I'm interested in a certain woman. To be honest, I was never very good at that courting stuff even in high school."

My mind began racing. Was he thinking of asking me out? How did I feel about that?

"And she's younger than me, too. So that makes it even harder. I don't want to look like an old fool."

I'm not much younger than you, I thought, regardless of what Benny just said. Libby, resting at my feet, rubbed her back against my leg as though to remind me she was happy with me just as I was.

"Any advice for me?" Jeff asked. "How is it done these days? I am so out of the loop. Did you know I lost my wife fifteen years ago? Cancer. Took a long time getting over that."

I reached across the table and touched his hand. "I'm sorry to hear that, I didn't know. I never married. You were lucky to have had that."

"Thank you, Jackie. But anyway, that leaves me here

in my sixties deciding how to ask this lady out. Any advice?"

"Just give that cute smile and ask."

"But she might shut me down."

"Guess you take that chance. Remember, we're not getting any younger."

Jeff grinned. "Really? You look younger every time I see you."

"I think small town life is agreeing with me," I said.

"You might be right. Just do it, huh?"

"Right," I said. Was this something I wanted with anyone here in Harmony? Jeff was handsome, a Jeff Bridges lookalike. He was kind, a solid guy, but I had so much on my plate right now. I'm just getting settled in. What would dating be like in such a small town? Everyone would know. Could we just stay casual? What if it didn't work out?

"These are great burgers. I heard they use high quality local beef. And local produce too."

"They are yummy." Why is he just eating his burger now? Was he too nervous to ask? I'd help him out. I tried to remember how to be coy. It had been a long time ago, but here goes.

"Who might this younger woman be?"

"Maybe I should wait to tell you until she accepts a date with me?" Jeff said. "Save face."

Okay... that didn't work. I'd try from another angle. "I'll bet she says yes," I said, trying to put on a suggestive smile.

"You do? Well, I'll tell you, but don't spread it around."

"Cross my heart," I answered.

CHAPTER THIRTEEN

"We met at your grand opening. Her name is Kay Whitlow. She owns the Whitlow Bed and Breakfast in town. Have you met her?"

I had to raise a napkin to my mouth to keep my choking covered up. You almost made a fool of yourself.

"You alright Jackie?"

I pretended to cough, giving myself time to recover my composure. "Just swallowed funny. Kay seems like a lovely woman. I did meet her briefly twice. Once at a Historical Society meeting and just this morning at Val's. I promise I won't say anything until I hear from you. But I don't know how she could turn you down."

Jeff blushed. "Now can I run some things by you about the Rick Ballard case?"

"Yes, please. I've discovered a few things I'd like to

tell you about too. First, I heard it's no longer just considered a suicide? There is a possibility he was murdered?"

"Well, there always was that possibility. And yes, I release you of your promise not to talk about it being suicide. I don't know why I ever assume things won't get around in our little community. We've expanded our investigation further. Financial irregularities seem to be a good motive. It appears there was a great deal of cutting costs and corners. Certain safety protocol was not put in place. Lots of the workers were complaining about that when I questioned them. Plus, grumbling about paychecks being late. One even said his bounced more than once."

"But wouldn't that point more to suicide? That Rick was afraid his fraudulent maneuverings were discovered, and he didn't want to face the music?"

"It might, but evidence at the scene told us there might be other possibilities. A blood spatter expert came in. He determined that the splatter patterns didn't fit with suicide. But the only prints on the gun were Rick's."

"Whoa. That changes things. What did Alan have to say?"

"Now that's what is so interesting. We haven't reached him yet. The camera at the site shows Alan driving away shortly after we saw you leave on the security video, so that all jibes. The security camera at the Riverview Motel shows him pulling up in the parking lot. He goes to his cabin, comes back out, and drives off."

"Which goes with what I was told. Are you sure it was him on the film?"

"Yes. Same basic build and that unusual limp. Plus, the timing fits. But then it's like he disappeared. This is all very suspicious. We have an all-points bulletin out on his vehicle. It hasn't been seen. I remembered you had some knowledge of him and his dealings in Chicago. Is there anything you can add that might help us find him?"

"I actually know little about him. Have you searched his cottage at the Riverview?"

"We did, and everything seemed normal. Wanda said he'd booked it for several days. I think his original plans were to check out on the weekend. His things were still in the cottage. Seemed like a messy guy though, like maybe he'd been looking for something before he left for Chicago. His clothes were still hanging in the closet and he left his toiletries. Not that unusual as he would have personal things back at his place in Chicago. We're bringing in a forensic accountant to take a dive into the books. Even if we haven't found Alan, we might find out if he was involved in financial fraud in any way."

"Like embezzlement?"

"Exactly," Jeff said. "The accountant hired by the investors was the one who suggested that he found many irregularities. He's willing to help our forensic accountant go through the books."

"But this doesn't make sense. Did you see Alan's car drive back in through the construction gate at any point?"

"No, but the accountant confirmed he was talking with both Alan and Rick at the construction trailer that night. They'd been arguing about money and management."

"That would have been what I overhead."

"Right. You told us you left on the golf cart after Rick gave Libby some water."

"I did. I didn't see the accountant that evening. I just wanted out of there at that point. It was so awkward. When I left, Alan was steaming mad. He was waiting to give Winford a lift back to the sales office where I guess he kept his bicycle. Is that what he takes to and from work?"

"It is. He's staying at Kay's B&B and that's where I went to question him Monday night. He confirmed what you said about that Sunday night argument. Apparently, he rides the trail from behind her house and then takes a side trail to get to the construction site. So that would be why we never saw him coming or going on any of the footage from the gate at the front of the site."

"So you see Alan leaving and this other guy leaves by some trail? Could he have been involved?"

"I don't think so," Jeff said. "Doesn't seem like he'd have it in him. Plus, he doesn't have a motive. Like I said, he works for the investors and pointed out that there was possible embezzlement going on prior to him arriving on the scene. He told me that his bosses are going to be in town this weekend. I imagine the pressure was on Rick and Alan."

"That might be why Alan got out of town so quickly. Did you check the airports? Maybe he skipped the country. But wait, if you didn't see Alan's car come back in, how could he have done it?"

"By the timing. We walked through the timeline of when you left. Alan had time to go back up and kill Rick. Winford Tarver told us that Alan was talking on his phone when he dropped him off at the sales office. Winford left on his bike and never saw Alan leave on the road out of the construction site. It appears that at some point, Alan unlocked and entered the sales office because Kim told us the lights were on in there in the morning when she opened up."

"I know someone you should talk to. His name is Rocco Montalvo."

"Is that the guy I found holding a suspect at gunpoint right on this patio?"

"The very same. He is staying on his boat at the marina. I think it might be a good idea to pay him a visit. I'll let him tell you how he's connected to Alan and Rick."

"Do you think Rocco might be a suspect?"

"Oh no, not that. He's a private investigator working for the investors. He has been for quite some time."

We ordered another round of beers. Benny came out and turned on the heat lamps as the patio was now in shadows from the hills that blocked the last sunlight.

It looked like it was clouding up too. I hoped the rain held off so we could take our time finishing our beers and enjoying the night air.

Through the large windows, I noticed Laura Lemke sat at a table just inside. The man she was with had his back to us. Laura looked like she was about ready to cry. Like she was just barely holding it together. She averted her eyes, not looking directly at her dining companion. When the waiter came over, Laura shook her head no at whatever he said. The man with her suddenly shoved his chair back. It hit against the pane of the window.

Jeff glanced over at the sudden sound. "That guy. What a jerk."

"Is that Tony Keaton?"

"Yes. His poor girlfriend. She's put up with him for too long."

"I heard he works at the construction site. Operating one of those pieces of heavy equipment."

"He does. We interviewed him Monday. Not a nice guy. He even claimed that Rick was hitting on his girl-friend. Can you believe it?"

"Hmm. She looks so sad. I met her briefly on Sunday, then she wasn't at work on Monday."

"Jackie, what are you thinking? I can see that look in your eyes."

"Might he be worth checking out further? Laura used to work with Val, and she witnessed just how crazy jealous Tony is."

"Oh, believe me, it crossed my mind. Did you see his car there?"

"No, but I saw something unusual from where I was taking sunset shots. A glint of sunlight hitting glass. And whatever it was, it seemed to be moving. I couldn't get a fix on it. Maybe Tony was hovering around? Hiding his presence until he knew everyone was gone but Rick. Waiting to confront him."

"When we gathered more information, I interviewed him again. He was there that night. He had lied earlier, saying Laura could give him an alibi."

My ears perked up. "You know, I saw him later at

Shorty's. He was drunk and belligerent. I imagine he knew his alibi was at risk of falling apart."

Jeff nodded. "Kim told us about Laura calling in on Monday. Red flags popped up all over, and Murph went over to see her. That poor girl. Anyway, let me give you Tony's story. He admitted he was waiting to confront Rick. That he saw you there at the construction trailer. He watched the three of you leave. He waited to make sure you were all gone. Remember, you can't see the sales office from the construction trailer, but when he thought Rick was the only one left on the property, he approached the trailer. Suddenly headlights coming up from below cut through the darkness. He quickly shut his own headlights off and backed away. He couldn't see who came driving up to the construction trailer from his vantage point. He heard a gunshot and the vehicle left. He claims he went up to the trailer, but now it was locked. Through the window he saw Rick in a pool of blood."

"Do you believe him? And did he show up on the gate camera?"

"He didn't show up on the camera. And the guy is a notorious liar. I'm keeping an eye on him. Like right now," Jeff said. He tipped his head toward the table inside the window where we saw Tony put his hand heavily on Laura's shoulder. She snapped her shoulder out from under his grasp, stood, and walked out of the Stone Mill.

Tony must have felt our stares because he shot a threatening look toward us before turning to follow Laura.

CHAPTER FOURTEEN

Mandy and I headed out for The Hills, where we knew Kim would be waiting. I hoped to see Laura this morning, but she was busy showing the model to someone. If I saw Tony as we made our way out into the construction area, I wanted it to be at a distance. The look he shot me last night chilled me. Did he know I was asking around about him?

Libby jumped into Kim's golf cart as though she owned it. "Hey wait a minute! That's my seat." I scooped her up and put her on my lap. Mandy climbed in the back seat and we were off.

"This is going to be so fun. I'm excited to add drone footage to our ad campaign. And what a gorgeous day for it," Kim said. "That rain last night is making the site a sloppy mess, but from the drone's sky view it'll still be beautiful. Jackie, have you talked to Stuart recently? He's been nervous about me being here. He thinks the protestors may do more than marching and chanting and waving signs. One of our guys found an encampment up in the hills above the future Driftless golf course. They might spy on our activity. I'm not afraid, but it rattles Stu with the things happening around here."

"Maybe the camp is just some kids setting up forts in the woods?" Mandy said. "We used to do that. We'd have bonfires and someone would bring a boom box for music."

I turned to look at her. "They still do that? We did that when I was a teenager too, except we'd have someone sneak in a few beers. And no boom boxes for us."

Kim burst out laughing! "I'm somewhere between you two in age, and we did the same thing!"

The ride with Kim was hair-raising. She took the turns and curves without slowing, even sliding through some. At least she'd slipped out of her high heels and into a pair of flats. "By Stuart's reporting, which will come out in Friday's edition of Harmony Happenings, it is much more than that. Luckily the guy who found it took photos before he called the police to report it. The squatters should have checked their plat maps, because voila, their camp was gone. It was on private property. Our property."

We slid to a stop near an unmarked van.

"How'd the drone guy make it up here in that big van?" Mandy asked.

"There is a temporary road cut in from the back of the property. It goes through someone's farm. We have permission to use it, but no one really knows about it. We're negotiating to buy the property, if our investors come through, that is. Now on to this adventure."

Kim was enthusiastic about most everything that involved her. As usual, she was perfectly made up and stylishly dressed. Today that meant slim ankle pants and a long-sleeved white linen tunic. How on earth she made it through the sloppy paths without a speck of mud on her was beyond me. Parts of the grounds were sand, but much of it was a reddish clay-like soil. In fact, as I got out, I noticed it on my pant legs from where I'd held Libby.

"Who knows about that back road?"

"Let me think…me, Rick, and now Dave the Drone Dude," Kim said. "He's getting a sign made for the side of his van. I've been helping him get a business plan together. First thing he needs is a sign for his van, I told him. Then a web page. And let me think who else knows. Of course, the farmer who owns the land. But we told him we don't want everyone and his brother using that road."

"You don't think the construction guys here would know about it?" I asked.

Kim shrugged. "I don't know about that. Why would they? They all come in through the gate and check in at the construction office. But some of them work on that far back end of things, so I suppose it's possible."

"If they all drive in through the front and check in at the construction trailer in the morning, how come no one discovered Rick's body earlier on Monday? I mean they arrive early, don't they?"

Kim had a quick answer for me. "The trailer was locked, so the guys just went to work and reported their time later that day. Well, I guess they didn't actually because later the police were there then. Hmm... I must have the new temporary foreman clear that up, so they don't miss their hours on the paycheck. Normally I'd say not my monkey, not my circus, but Scott has his hands full as it is."

"He's the new temporary foreman?" I asked.

It was Mandy who answered. "He's just taking it on for a week or two because he's familiar with construction and the paperwork."

"I suggested him," Kim quickly added. "With

everyone running around like chickens with their heads cut off someone had to settle this place down."

Dave the Drone Dude had already launched his drone. We were mesmerized watching the landscape below come alive on the screen in front of us.

"This is unbelievable. I think I'll have to get one of these toys for Matt for Christmas," Mandy said.

"Hey, I know Matt, Matt Drake, right? We were buddies in high school," Dave said.

"That's right. What's your last name? I'll tell him we met."

"Here's my business card," Dave said, as he carefully held the controller and reached in his pocket. "Besides buying the drone, and the van, at least I got these printed up."

Mandy said, "Kim was saying you could use some help with your website. Matt has built a couple. One for his dad's construction business and one for the photography studio. And now he's building one for Patti's catering business too. Maybe you two could work out a barter agreement. Drone lessons for a website?"

"Cool. Have him call me. Tell him I'll buy him a beer and we can talk."

"Well Dave, I'm very impressed with your expertise with videotaping using the drone. Is the editing program easy to learn?" I asked.

"This whole thing has been a steep learning curve, but with just word of mouth I'm almost ready to quit my other job."

All the while we'd been chatting, I was keeping my eyes on the screen. "Your maneuvering skills are top-notch. And maybe the ad agency will do the editing as they choose. What format do you use for output?"

I heard Dave answer me, but it didn't register because of something I thought I saw on the screen. "Dave, can you fly back slowly over that part again? I thought I caught something very odd looking."

"Sure. When you see the area you want to examine closer, I'll drop down and hover so just point on the screen."

I think Dave made out what I was seeing because without me saying anything more he lowered the drone, closer and closer to a shallow excavation. Water that had collected in the bottom must have lifted the body floating there.

one of us had a good cell phone signal here to call in what we were seeing. A body, and now someone preparing to fill in the excavated ground with dirt. We had to stop them.

All four of us called out, screaming *STOP* at the top of our lungs. Libby caught the panicked feeling and began barking loudly.

But all to no avail.

We were too far away.

The equipment was too loud.

The operator didn't hear us.

We watched in horror as the big earth moving equipment pushed a huge mound of dirt closer and closer to the edge. With one last shove, a rolling pile of rock and gravel covered the body.

We all gasped.

"Come on Kim, we've got to stop them," I shouted.

"You all go ahead," Dave said. "I'll keep the drone up so you can see where the body was."

"Good idea, Dave," Mandy said.

Kim, Mandy, Libby and I hurried to the golf cart and raced back downhill to the construction site. We kept the drone in our sights. It helped us locate the site quickly. Kim jumped out, wildly waving her arms and shouting to get the operator's attention.

Finally, after moving another big mound of dirt over the body that he obviously couldn't see from his position, the operator stopped, pulled headphones off and leaned out to shout. "Watch out lady! Damn, I almost backed into you. What the heck are you doing out here?"

He stepped out.

It was Tony.

Kim glared at him, her knuckles tight against her hips. "Don't yell at me young man. There's a body in that pit you're filling in. Couldn't you see that?"

Tony waved Kim off. "That's BS. Get out of here. I can't see into the pit from my seat. Now get out of my way, before you accidentally fall in. I'm behind. This was to be done Monday." He climbed back into the bulldozer's seat and shifted into gear.

Kim moved closer. "Just look, you idiot!"

Tony slammed the gears, jumped out of the dozer, stomped to the edge of the pit, and looked in. Then with a rude hand gesture, he ran back to the machine and started it moving again.

Libby leaped out and yelped aggressively at him. Even charging the edge of his blade equipment.

Mandy screamed. "No, Libby. Come Libby. Stop Libby."

I couldn't watch anymore. I ran toward the bulldozer where I knew Tony could see me. He stopped the equipment, but threateningly revved the engine.

I held up one hand and called to Mandy. "Grab Libby." She ran toward Libby, holding out a treat she always kept in her pocket. Libby saw that and ran to her. I gave Tony a thumbs up, and he resumed filling the hole.

Kim shouted at me. "What are you doing, Jackie? He's burying a body, for god's sake."

"Kim, can't you see that we can't make him stop? Of course, he can't see the body now, he already put dirt on top of It. He's not going to believe us. Let's go find Scott at the construction trailer. He'll have a walkie talkie and can order him to halt."

Jumping back in the golf cart, we raced away toward the construction trailer area, knowing Tony would keep filling in the pit, but it could be dug out. We were only putting ourselves in danger out there.

Scott heard us out and immediately reached Tony. We heard them arguing over the company's radio. Eventually Tony did stop, but he was not happy about Scott bossing him around.

"Okay now, you're sure this is a body? Seeing it from the drone high in the sky, it could have been part of a tree with limbs sticking out," Scott suggested.

"Scott, the drone hovered closely over the body. In fact, we're sure that's what it was. How fast can you get excavation equipment to that pit?"

"Assuming the person is dead and I'm not talking about a rescue, I'll pull Craig off his job and have him take an excavator out there. But if you think the person might still be alive, I'll send the crew with shovels and the smaller bobcat to save him. He might have a pocket of air to breathe."

Kim and Mandy looked at me. I knew what they were thinking. Could the person possibly have been alive, and we left Tony to push more dirt on top of him? But I knew, from our first sight of the grotesque body. He was dead.

I finally took the lead. "He's dead, but we want to be careful uncovering him in case there's evidence of wrongdoing."

Scott made some more calls on his radio and we all left for the site where the body was buried.

The slow and careful excavation revealed the body of Alan Morris. It had been in this pit for days by the condition of it. The medical examiner arrived on scene, as did Chief Jeff and Murph.

The examiner was left with a body several days old, rain soaked, and then buried by tons of rock and soil. "This is going to be a hard case. He could have accidentally fallen in here. No obvious gunshot wounds. The injuries to the body caused by it being buried today would not have caused bruising, only surface abrasions. We'll do the autopsy and hopefully find a cause of death."

"Could he have been buried at a shallow depth earlier?" I ask.

"What makes you say that?" the examiner, our own local doctor, Dawn Trueblood asked.

"When we first saw it and Dave began lowering the drone, there was soil on top of the body. I believe the drone footage will verify what I remember seeing. That's when the thought that the water had caused him to float up crossed my mind."

Jeff said, "Good point. We'll check that out. Our officer is with Dave now and they are working on getting the clips out of the longer video so we can examine them."

As we all stood looking down at the body of Alan Morris, Jeff said, "And he might have been buried in here for all eternity if not for the rain. We checked out the angle and Tony operating the dozer wouldn't have seen the body."

I said, "Luckily the rain made him a floater, but if not for the drone and us seeing him, he would have been buried again, this time by Tony."

I paused and waited to see if what I just said had sunk in with Chief Jeff. It had.

"Can we see the schedule of work assignments for this area?" Jeff asked Scott.

Scott said, "I only stepped in yesterday as you know, so I'm not up to speed on the scheduling. I'll try to help as best I can."

"Thanks, Scott," Jeff said. "First thing I want to know is when was this pit dug and what other activity was scheduled around here, including today."

"I'll look into that for you," Scott answered.

Tony stood to one side, watching us. He unnerved me. And with what I knew about how he treated women, I couldn't wait to get out of his presence.

"Jackie, can you stop by my office later when I have those video clips?" Jeff asked me.

"Sure," I answered.

Jeff turned back to look at the body. "Alan was around when Paul Griffin died, and the same with Luella Hagge's death. He was my prime suspect in Rick Ballard's death. But now it's looking like I won't be able to prove he did it."

They brought the body up on a stretcher, though navigating through the still muddy ground wasn't easy.

Jeff told Scott and Tony that they would search the site for any other evidence, and it was not to be disturbed further. Tony, who had been leaning on his equipment, mumbled some unpleasant sounding words and said, "Yes, boss," in a mocking tone.

Everyone was leaving. Kim and Mandy climbed back into the golf cart. Scott pulled me aside as I headed that way too.

"Jackie, can we meet tonight? I have something I want to run by you," he said.

Oh gosh, this sounds familiar. Now I'll have Scott asking me for dating advice too. Maybe when he did Kay's remodeling, he found himself attracted to her. I hope he didn't want to go to the Stone Mill Brewery. That would be too much for even me to take.

"Sure, where should we meet?"

"I'd like this to be private. Can I come by your place say around nine?"

. . .

The word about the discovery of the body of Alan Morris spread like wildfire through Harmony.

Stuart called me before Mandy and I even got back to town. Of course, he wanted as much information as he could get. He had already connected with Dave the drone guy and hoped to get a still shot of what we had all seen. "Though of course I won't show the body, that would be too graphic. I can blur it out. But I think the drone angle will make it an interesting story. As to background information on Alan, I probably have enough from those other two cases," Stuart said.

"I don't think there's much more I can tell you, Stuart. Kim was right there with us the whole time," I said.

"Wasn't Alan becoming the primary suspect in Rick's murder?" Stuart asked.

I wasn't sure how to answer, but Jeff had said it out loud in front of us all, so I agreed. "He was and may still be. After all, we saw Alan leaving the site on Sunday night."

"Then how did he end up back in a hole in the ground there today?" Stuart asked. "This is getting interesting. Maybe Chief Jeff should bring in help. Like that

Detective Louise Taylor from the County Sheriff's Department."

"The body was just discovered, and I think we should give Jeff time to investigate. I mean, he could have come back and accidentally fallen in and knocked his head. They'll be checking the camera footage again to see if he returned to the job site."

"Was his car there?"

"I don't think so. Good point, Stuart."

"Those darn protestors could have done something. They've been vandalizing the site. Even some of the equipment there. Maybe Alan was staking them out, and they discovered it and pushed him into the hole and stole his car."

"Come on, Stuart. Don't go all goofy on this. Let's see what Jeff discovers."

Stuart laughed. "Jackie, I'm an investigative reporter and we seek information."

"True. But what information do you have that protestors would go that far?" I asked him.

"Kim told me about an encampment above the construction site. Maybe Alan heard about it and went there to check it out. The protestors knocked him out. Dumped his body in the pit and took his car and hid it somewhere. Or took it to Cutter's Salvage Yard for some money to fund their cause."

"But don't forget, Stuart. Alan left for Chicago on Sunday night. But that's not been verified. He's not checked back into his room at the Riverview since then either."

Stuart pondered that for a few moments. "And hasn't returned calls, correct?"

"Right."

"And they haven't found his car, right?"

"Right. So how does that possibly fit in with the protestors at a hidden encampment in the forest, killing him and burying his body?"

Stuart said, "Consider this. Alan came back to Harmony on let's say Monday afternoon, and before going to the motel, went to check the tent city out."

"But then they would have seen him on the site camera."

"Oh Jackie, think about that. He could have simply used that back road."

"How do you know about the back road?" I asked.

"Kim told me. Alan learned about the encampment and the back road."

"Stuart Walters, you have piqued my curiosity. I like the way you think!"

. . .

*J*eff called late in the afternoon, and I went to look at the videos again with him. "This technology is really booming. I've heard of cases of missing persons found using heat seeking technology in drones," Jeff said. "I agree with what you said, that had Tony kept filling that shallow pit, we'd never have found the body. It's such an enormous site and we might not even have thought to look for Alan Morris there."

"I know. It's strange," I said.

"I'd like to stop at the first moment you saw what looked like a body. I mean, how did you even make that out?" Jeff asked.

I found and froze the frame on the moment Jeff wanted to see. "It's probably part of my attention to detail in my work. I just was absorbed in watching the video when something clicked and I asked him to fly the drone back over. This is what we saw. Now let it go to the point where it's a closer shot. Do you see what I mean? Doesn't the body appear to have dirt on it?"

"It does. But the water might have washed some dirt over on top of it."

"I suppose that's possible. But I think it's something to keep in mind as you investigate this. Someone might have tried to hide the body in a shallow grave. He could have known this was a place that would eventually be covered over."

Jeff pinched his nose bridge with his fingers. "I know what you're suggesting. I'm waiting on Scott's scheduling answers. You think Tony may have been there today because he knew what needed to be done."

"It is possible. I can't put all the pieces together, but I do know how Tony could get in without being caught on camera. There is a back road. An entrance no one really uses. Just a right of way now, but the company will be purchasing it. Alan could have used it. And Tony as well. That would explain how he could have been there on Sunday night without going through the front gate."

"He mentioned something about using that road to sneak in," Jeff said. "I'll have to check that out."

"Jeff, Stuart and Kim brought up the protestors. They had an encampment in the hills. Apparently, it's been broken up, so you probably know about it. Do you think those protestors that have been causing trouble on the site could have had a hand in any of this?"

"I know nothing about it. I'll reach out to the County Sheriff's Department, because that encampment was probably out of the city limits and they may have broken it up. Then I'll have Kim show me where the road is. And maybe I'll hear from Scott shortly too. Things are heating up."

CHAPTER SIXTEEN

After talking with Jeff this afternoon about all the twists and turns in the two murder cases, I needed a break.

Badly!

When the call came to join Aunt Ruth at Shady Pines for their first Wednesday of the month potluck dinner, I quickly accepted. That worked out perfectly as Scott couldn't meet until later and I welcomed the distraction of their company.

The cloth covered picnic table groaned under the weight of the baked dishes, pasta salads, cold cuts, jello, brownies, and assorted cheeses in plastic containers. Or in Corningware with the original corn-flower posies from the fifties. Dishes that would have been in families for decades.

I saw Aunt Ruth and her friends saved me a chair near their table. I decided I might as well load up my plate before heading over to join them. Chatter and laughter carried through the early evening air, mixed in with someone calling out bingo numbers by the community center. A celebratory mood permeated this place. I prayed Aunt Ruth could live out the rest of her life in her little cottage. Now that I made my home in Harmony, I'd be around to help her as she aged.

"Well lookie who's here!" a man said as I approached the gal's table. "Remember me? We met at the Historical Society meeting right after that kerfuffle with the dead lady."

"For god's sake, Elmer. How can you call someone's death a kerfuffle?"

"Sure felt like it to me," Elmer said.

"Depends how you define that word," Betty said. "Now I consider it to mean..."

Dorothy rolled her eyes. "Can we let Jackie sit down and eat her dinner?"

I opened up the folding lawn chair and sat down, carefully balancing my plate on my lap. "I do remember you, Elmer. And you as well, Harry. Nice to see you both again. Do you live here in Shady Pines?"

Harry grunted what I took for a yes, and Elmer nodded. "We both do. All the cabins are filled up now."

"How many times do I have to tell you these are cottages? They were cabins when this was a Lutheran summer camp," Eunice said.

"Well excuse me," Elmer said. "All the cottages are presently occupied by old codgers." He threw a smirk in Eunice's direction.

"Bound to be turnover after summer," Harry mumbled.

"Why are you so morbid?" Eunice said. "Turnover my pituddy. This is it. No more deaths in Harmony until next year."

"Especially since they found another body," Betty said. "That would seem to fill any quotient expected from our little village, don't you think?"

Harry slowly stroked his beard. "I'm good with that. But just sayin' odds are that…"

"Zip your lip, Harry," Eunice said. "We're eating supper."

"Jackie dear," Aunt Ruth said. "Without getting into any gritty details, can you tell us what happened today? I understand you discovered the body. From an airplane or something like that."

"It was a drone, Auntie. Kim hired this kid to fly a drone, with a video camera attached, to demonstrate the possibilities for advertising. We were watching his video screen and saw a shape that looked like a body. Turns out it was Alan Morris."

Dorothy let out a big sigh. "Amazing what technology can do. That body might not have been discovered for weeks."

"That's absolutely right. Maybe never. The bulldozer operator was getting ready to fill in the excavated area."

"Numb-skull," Harry mumbled.

"In fairness, Tony couldn't see what was in the pit from his dozer seat," I said.

"We heard that the investors are coming in this weekend because there are irregularities with the finances. Might that have something to do with the murders?" Betty asked. "I watch Murder She Wrote reruns and so very many times the motive is money. Always need a motive!"

"That could be the case here," I said.

"Say, how are the photographs for the garment book coming along?" Ruth asked. "We are eager to help you with it."

"If any of you would like to join us, I'm meeting Hannah tomorrow morning," I said.

"We'll be there too," Dorothy said. "We're working on digging through old photographs and documents. Hannah has set us up in some third-floor rooms so we can do our research. Some days we work at the library, acquiring information from the newspapers on file there. You should see what they used to print up. So and so went to Chicago and wore the special gown she had made in New York. They described the attire of guests at weddings in great detail. Really quite interesting."

"Not like that skinny four-page thing they call a paper now," Harry said.

Ruth pinched her lips and said, "Harry, must you always be such a curmudgeon? We are lucky to have Stuart Walters in our village. He is the only person who took on the Harmony Happenings and is probably not making a dime on it. Don't you dare speak like that!"

Harry snickered. "He doesn't need to. His wife supports him."

Aunt Ruth clicked her tongue and stood to clear some of our dishes. Putting an effort toward not say anything more. At this age, people are set in their ways. Ruth was too smart of a lady to get sucked into pointless arguing with an old man.

"Question for you all. Remember Monday night when I walked the Go Round Trail? I saw an old abandoned farm up top of the hill in that direction." I pointed in the direction I calculated the place might be.

"Gunkel place maybe," Elmer offered. "But I think the old lady still lives there."

"Her kids moved out west to South Dakota and rarely visit. I'm glad the pastor checks in on her," Ruth said. "But Jackie, there are many abandoned farms out that way."

Harry stood, adjusting his suspenders. "I'll get my plat book."

"Thanks, Harry," I said.

"From my cabin..." he said under his breath.

"Goofy old man," Eunice retorted. "Why do you want to know, Jackie?"

"I left the trail, and I caught a glimpse of it. I've always wanted to photograph abandoned farmhouses and barns. Homesteads that have sat empty. I saw this one from the trail, but I want to see how to get there by car. And of course, I'll want to find the owners to get permission."

"Well, we've got a lot of those places in Wisconsin. Probably across the Midwest, in fact. Now they've started what they call deconstructing them. Taking them apart instead of just letting them crumble and collapse in on themselves," Dorothy said.

"They make me sad," Betty said.

Ruth agreed. "I don't need to think about all that loss. No one wanting to take the place over. Renting the fields out. And like Grace Gunkel, just living in a smaller and smaller space in an almost empty house." She shivered slightly and looked out across the grounds with something on her mind. Maybe what I'd been thinking.

The move from the apartment had been stressful, I'm sure. So many memories for her there.

That reminded me of something. "Ruth, did you get the rest of those film rolls developed?"

"Here comes Harry with his plat book," Ruth said, deftly avoiding my question.

A plat book shows land plats, pieces of property, and who owns them. The book Harry brought out to us was for this county.

"These are 'bout ten years old, but those pieces of old farm properties are probably owned by the same family."

Elmer pulled a pen from his shirt pocket protector and used it to point to the graveyard as a starting point. Everyone had differing opinions of where the trail ran, and soon we had a small crowd gathered around our table. People began offering suggestions, with ideas tossed around willy-nilly. My only real reference point was the graveyard. I remembered the trail map in my phone and brought that up, which helped. You could have filled a display rack with all the reading glasses brought out to peer at my phone and at the maps in Harry's plat book.

I tried pulling up the satellite map on my phone too, but there were so many trees that many of the curvy roads up in the hills were obscured.

Finally, it appeared we'd nailed it down to two possible plots of land. One was owned by the Crankshaw family and the other by the name of Woller.

"Does anyone know a contact for these people?"

"Old man Crankshaw is renting out his barn to horse people, I think," Dorothy said.

"And isn't Patti at the village hall one of the Woller girls? She might be a contact for that place."

"Great. Thanks so much." I took a photo of the plat map with my phone as it showed the roads as well. It couldn't be the horse farm place, but it might be the old Woller farm. Hopefully Patti could help me with that.

I looked around the group gathered here. I was happy for Ruth to be among people her own age. But one thing troubled me. Why was she avoiding showing me those old photos? Guess they were probably nothing. But the more she avoided the subject the more I wanted to know.

s soon as I left Shady Pines, I called Patti and asked about the farm.

"Yes, that was my grandparents' place. My sisters and I used to stay there. I have such fond memories of it, like playing dress up with all the treasures we girls discovered in the attic. The sweet fragrance of the apple orchard. The dim stuffiness of the henhouse when Grandma sent us out to collect eggs for breakfast. But why are you asking about it, Jackie?"

"I'd like to have your permission, along with good directions, to go there and take photographs. I noticed the property line runs along near the Go Round Trail. I walked it on Monday and took a short sidewalk to your family's farm. I saw it was abandoned but didn't want to disturb the place. Plus, if these photos come together in a book someday, I'll need permission to publish them."

I heard a soft chuckle come over the phone connection. "It's not completely abandoned though, Jackie. The buildings might be, but you must not have seen the rather substantial garden I have there."

"Really? No, I didn't see that."

"I was out there last Sunday, but I do need to go again tomorrow and do some more watering. I get water from the still functioning hand-dug well. The old iron hand pump works fine after all these years. Want to meet me there later? I was planning to do a midweek watering."

"That would be perfect, Patti. I have an appointment in the morning. What time were you going?"

"Tell you what, I'll call when I'm leaving. Joyce holds down the fort at the Village Hall whenever I need to slip out."

"Okay. I'll see you tomorrow. Thanks."

"Wait, Jackie. You're not getting off that easy. Is it true that you discovered yet another body?"

"How about we talk about it tomorrow, Patti? I'll fill you in then."

"I'll hold you to that!"

· · ·

I puttered downstairs in the studio as the twilight descended, working on the computer and waiting for Scott to arrive. Running a business like this differed greatly from my J.P. Photography business. With that, I had no brick-and-mortar site. No electric or water bill. No employees' paychecks. No building maintenance. I was absorbed in clearing out old emails when the knock on the front door startled me.

Scott stood there holding up a wine bottle and a small box.

I unlocked the door for him.

He greeted me. "I come bearing gifts from the new wine and cheese shop. My first foray into choosing a food and wine pairing," he said. Then with a wink added, "Don't worry, the clerk helped me out."

"My goodness, I wasn't expecting all of this."

"I didn't want to come empty-handed since I sort of invited myself over."

"Come on. Let me shut down things here and we'll go to the balcony upstairs. It's the perfect night for it."

After lighting a candle and putting the cheese slices on a wooden board with a small bunch of grapes, I poured us each a glass of wine. We toasted to the half-moon appearing in the sky and to my new place.

"You said you had something you wanted to ask me about," I crossed my toes it wasn't another ask like Jeff's.

It wasn't.

"Jackie, I need your advice about taking my suspicions to the police. Or to just keep my nose out of it. Mandy seems to believe you have good instincts about things. I was telling her and my son about a situation that came up in my new, and gratefully temporary role as construction foreman. Mandy said the best idea would be to come to you."

Well, I have to admit to myself that question deflated my bubble a little. And I had to smile when even Libby lifted her head and tilted it with that quizzical look at Scott.

"I'm not sure if my answer or advice will carry any weight but go ahead."

"You found the body and were there when they were investigating Rick's death, so I think it does," Scott said. He took a sip of wine. "Do you like this? I know little about wine but wouldn't mind learning. Expand my horizons and all that."

"To be honest, I'm not a wine connoisseur either."

"I thought, being a world traveler and all, you would have had the knowledge and experience that a small-town blue-collar guy sorely lacks."

"Scott, you'd be surprised. I've always felt awkward when put in situations where I'm asked to take the sample sip and see if a bottle of wine is okay."

"From the guy with the towel over his arm?" Scott said.

"Yes. First lesson, he's called a sommelier. And he may have spent hundreds of hours learning about wines, so with him watching me I'd want to appear wise and worldly. But I'm not. And have never had a burning desire to learn either. I'm okay with passing off the choosing and sampling to someone else."

"Like the sommelier?"

"Or my dinner companion. Or, in a wine and cheese shop, the store clerk!"

"So, I did good?"

"You did, Scott. And the clerk knows her stuff, this tastes delicious."

"I'm enjoying it too," Scott said, with that low Sam Elliott tone of his voice. "But for me many meals, or perhaps in this case wines, taste good but are memorable because of the company and the ambiance. You can't beat this little cozy balcony, the view over the green lawns of the park, and the moon's reflection on the river."

I looked across the candlelight at Scott and silently

agreed with him, even as I reached down to stroke Libby's head.

Scott smiled. "But now Jackie, on to my reason for coming here. I am finding out things about this construction operation that are troubling. I'm not handling any finances but am receiving orders made previously and the PO's don't seem to match up with what I see coming in. Also, I can tell they have used low grades of concrete for the intended purpose. I know I'm not familiar with commercial projects, but I recognize inferior concrete when I see it. I spoke to Winford Tarver, the accountant there, and he's well aware that there appear to be what he calls troubling irregularities. He asked me to keep him in my loop of what I come across as he is building a report to turn over to the investor group. Okay, so I delegated those concerns to him, and he seems on top of it. But the thing I'm bringing to you is what really troubles me. When Alan Morris's body was discovered, you reached out to me to stop the worker who was filling in that excavated site."

"Right, Tony Keaton. He told me it was on his work schedule. He would have driven his bulldozer over there and just started shoving dirt in as per schedule."

Scott nodded thoughtfully. "That's the sense I got. But some other guys said that wasn't where he was supposed to be."

"Did you find the schedules that Jeff asked about?"

"No. I couldn't make heads or tails out of the papers Rick left. I'm not used to the scale they worked with. So, I asked some guys to help. That's how I discovered the possibility that Tony was in the wrong area. He denied it and said he was just finishing up something he didn't get to on Monday. I'm not comfortable saying this, but do you think he knew the body was there, and he purposely thought he'd quick cover it up?"

I wasn't completely shocked by that thought. "When we saw he was pushing more dirt over the body, we raced down to stop him. He seemed angry about it. In fact, that's when I backed off and came to you. Also, it appears the body had been covered, buried if you will, but rains filled the pit and the body floated up. Are you asking if he might have murdered Alan Morris?"

"And maybe Rick? I guess I am. Or, and this sounds weird, Tony was told, or hired, to do it. Now here I go even weirder. Was he reassigned to that part of the job by someone else to trick him?"

"That's thinking outside the box, Scott," I said. "Good job."

"You're kidding right?" Scott looked stunned. "That I would try to connect some kid my son's own age to a murder. I'm afraid that even sitting here someone might be underneath us listening and the rumors will start flying. That's the reason I tried to keep this conversation private."

"I know what you mean about rumors. But no, what I admire about the way you think is that you don't just see and say. You think further. Like if this, then what about that? You explore the gray area between the black and the white."

"So where does that leave me with the situation at hand? Might this just be guys trying to get Tony in trouble because he's such a pain in the butt?" Scott asked.

"Can you put this on pause for tonight? Like you said, the financial issues are one thing, but relationships between coworkers can get nasty. Did you know Tony's girlfriend Laura works in the sales office with Kim?"

"I didn't. And I would love to put it on pause for tonight. But I want Jeff to know what I'm hearing from the site. I wish I'd never agreed to take this on. And I can't wait until my tour of duty in that war zone is over. Will you be talking to Jeff tomorrow?" Scott asked.

"I might be. Why?"

Scott tipped his head and grinned. "He seems to enjoy having you involved with his cases. I'm just hoping that the only reason is because you have a curious, inquisitive mind."

"And a clever one, too?" I smiled. "Is telling me this

about the murder the only reason you wanted to meet on my balcony?"

"No. I also wanted to have the right ambiance to enjoy my big foray into choosing wines. Cheers, Jackie."

I raised my wineglass. "Cheers, Scott."

CHAPTER EIGHTEEN

Thursday morning found me at the Harmony House, now called the Harmony Museum and Nature Center after Eleanor Harmony donated it to the village. The family home of the village's founding family, the mansion Gustave Harmony built, was now a place to hold the historical memorabilia of this area of southwest Wisconsin. The beautiful grounds surrounding it provided an outdoor place for education and special events.

It was also the scene of the murder of Luella Hagge, the head of Building and Zoning who'd given Alan Morris and his associates such a bad time with permitting and inspections.

But nothing is going to diminish my happiness today. I slept well last night after that nice evening with

Scott. I was glad we didn't go out, instead enjoying my little balcony.

I was early for my appointment with Hannah regarding the fashion book, so I decided to see how the grounds and nature center were coming along.

The progress was impressive. With the warm weather and recent rains, everything was greening up nicely. Small signposts were unobtrusively tucked in among the low plantings or mounted on slender posts next to the taller plants and trees, identifying the common name and the scientific name for the many school children who would be visiting this nature center. Benches were scattered on the walkways and grounds, an invitation to sit for a spell and enjoy Mother Nature's show.

Occasional arbors scattered over the landscape, scaled and broke up the open areas into room-like gardens. Vines climbed up a two-story trellis attached to the mansion, remaining much as they had the night I discovered them...and Luella Hagge's body.

Birds called out across the grounds. I took the time to look more closely. It surprised me to see so many bird feeders scattered throughout the area. My goodness, what a job to keep those feeders full, but what pleasure it gave those who walked here.

I was pleasantly surprised to see Tom and Eleanor

strolling on the walkway. "Hello there, you two. What a lovely morning!" I called out.

"Jackie, it's wonderful to run into you here. Tom and I often come up the hill and stroll the grounds," Eleanor said. "Have you seen the amazing job the landscapers have done? They kept much of what Tom had nurtured over the years but are filling in with delightful new species."

"Do you miss working here, Tom? You had such a knack for it," I asked.

Tom took Eleanor's arm, tucking it into his. "We are honorary members here and I love seeing it develop. But you must check out what we've been doing at the Mill House now, too. It's a much more manageable task to keep up the landscaping there. This place was getting to be way too much for me after I entered my eighties. Now I get to enjoy this lovely lady's company as she helps me at our new home."

Eleanor's laughter had such a joyful ring to it. "Who knew I'd enjoy gardening? I never tried it before, and I just love it. But like Tom says, in the right amount. What are you doing here, Jackie? Just checking it out?"

"That, and I'm meeting Hannah about documenting your generous donation of the garments your family preserved over the years. I got a peek at them at the fundraising gala, but we'll be going into more depth today. I'm super excited about the book we'll be putting together. I imagine it will be a good sell locally but also across the country. From what Hannah says, it's an extraordinary collection."

"I've shared my memories of the women in my family who wore the things with her, but please don't hesitate to ask me anything at all. I just know when they are put on mannequins and brought to life in your photographs, more memories will return."

"So how have you been, Jackie?" Tom asked. "Eleanor and I want to congratulate you on the taking over the business. We haven't been to see the new studio. Or is it a gallery?" Tom said.

"Thank you so much. It's a combination sort of place, I guess. I'll have rotating displays by photographers from outside the area. There are some Chicago friends exhibiting their work now. We'll still do sittings and events and see how much of a market is here for that. I've been working with training Mandy Drake. She's great! She also is offering custom framing with an emphasis on reusing old frames."

"I bet she's looking forward to the antique market coming. Hannah is organizing it for an event to show-case the Museum and promote Harmony. Mandy will be sure to find some good frames there."

"I heard something about that. I think it sounds like a great idea," I said.

"Speaking of that, my great-niece Laura works in the sales office for the resort. She's excited about more people coming to town. I think she mentioned something about having a table at the market to promote the resort," Tom said.

"Say Jackie," Eleanor asked. "Was there another murder at the resort? We read the Harmony Happenings on Tuesday about the construction foreman. But then we overheard someone saying there was a body found buried on the site somewhere. Or are we just mixing up stories?"

"You're not mixing up stories. The man they found was Paul's former partner, Alan Morris."

Eleanor gasped, and Tom wrapped his arm around her to support her. "Oh, no. What on earth happened? Poor Alan."

"This was just discovered yesterday morning. I was watching a demonstration by a drone pilot and we spotted the body from a flyover shot. We raced down to stop a construction worker from moving dirt on top of the body."

"My goodness. Do they have any idea how he was murdered?"

"Not that I know of. It's still early in the investigation."

Tom was shaking his head. "What about that Rick guy who was killed? The article seemed to suggest it was a suicide."

"It's a murder investigation. The blood spatter expert said his findings didn't jibe with the suicide theory."

Tom and Eleanor exchanged a meaningful glance and Tom nodded. Eleanor said, "When we saw the name of the man, Rick Ballard, it immediately raised a flag for Tom and I."

She looked at Tom again. He said, "Go ahead, you might be better at telling the story."

"Tom is particularly close to his great-niece, Laura. On Sunday, in the early evening, she came to us. She'd been hurt, Jackie. You could see the bruising starting to show on her arms and even," Eleanor struggled to continue so Tom spoke.

"It looked like she had been punched in the face. It was her boyfriend. She came to us because she knew her parents would call the police on him. She didn't want to see him thrown in jail. But I can tell you, if I was twenty years younger, I'd punch the guy's lights out."

"Tom, was it Tony Keaton who hit her?"

"You know him then?"

"I've met him. He was the worker shoving the dirt over Alan's body. That's worded wrong. He was operating equipment and from his seat inside the bulldozer he couldn't see into the pit but was moving earth to fill in the area where we'd seen Alan's body."

"So, he was covering up a crime scene?"

"Not exactly, that's why I have to be careful with my words while the investigation is ongoing."

Eleanor spoke. "Understood. We were just so disturbed by Laura's story on Sunday night. And I'm still on edge."

"I'm sorry to hear about Laura, I know she didn't come to work Monday morning. What you just told me would explain that. But why did Rick's death raise a flag for you about Tony and Laura?"

"Because, between sobs, Laura told us why Tony had been especially upset Sunday. They'd argued about Rick Ballard. It started in the morning and Tony was drinking, so it escalated. Laura said Rick Ballard sensed tension between her and Tony on the job site, and he asked her if Tony was verbally abusing her. She confided in him about Tony's temper. Apparently, Tony saw them talking, and he read it as Rick was hitting on Laura. She couldn't convince him otherwise," Tom said.

Eleanor added, "Please don't think we tell you this lightly. You were so helpful to me when Paul died. And I feel running into you here today was meant to be. If you think this information is of consequence, please let

Chief Jeff know. We don't want to put Laura in a bad spot about it, so we'd appreciate you being as discreet as you can."

"Certainly, I'll talk to Jeff and share your story and your request. But it might come to him interviewing Laura. I'm sure he could do it without Tony being made aware. Now will you do me a favor? Insist Laura get out of that situation. Before she gets worse than a black eye."

I couldn't shake what I'd heard from Eleanor and Tom. This made me even more concerned that Tony was Rick's murderer. It would be easy enough to wipe fingerprints off a gun and put the dead man's on it.

"Jackie, you seem distracted," Hannah said. "Is something wrong?"

"No, just heard something that might be pertinent to Rick Ballard's death. Sorry. I'll put it on the back burner and give you my undivided attention."

We were in a second-floor room of the Harmony Mansion that Hannah was proposing I use as a studio, saying I should set up my backdrops and lightening, leaving them here until the process was complete.

She'd already brought old dressmaker forms in to use as frames to put the garments on. This would be sweet to set up a properly lit and draped setting that could stay in place for weeks or months for consistency in the way the garments' photographs look. I pictured a simple backdrop so I could highlight the details of the various pieces.

"That would be great," I told Hannah. "And we could encourage tourists to observe us working on preserving the garments on film. If any student groups come through, I'd be happy to give them brief talks on photography as well."

"That's very generous of you. We still have 4-H clubs here, and I know there's both a sewing component and a photography one. It would be a wonderful experience for them. Come on, let's go up to the third floor. Some committee members are working up there. We've got a treasure trove of photographs to go through as well. We're trying to match them up with diaries and journals. And then finally with garments."

As we climbed the back staircase, my mind flashed to the night of Luella Hagge's murder. What stories these servant stairs could tell. The back staircase started in the kitchen and continued up to the third floor. It was used to carry midnight snacks or evening tea to the bedrooms and sitting areas, as well as freshly laundered linens on wash day.

It also was the staircase used for the staff to retire to

their third-floor bedrooms at night. Some were young girls hired to do laundry and ironing who might return home to family on the weekends. Others were maids and cooks who chose to live here. I'd been told by Hannah that some third-floor rooms were used to store household items, like out of season decorations as well.

I heard them laughing and chattering before we even got to the door of one room. A large table took over almost the entire modest bedroom. Dorothy and Ruth sat at the table which held photograph albums and unmounted photos in small boxes. Across the hall, Betty and Eunice were seated at a similar table, attaching sticky notes to what appeared to be handwritten letters.

"How is it going, ladies?" Hannah asked.

Betty waved a letter in the air. "This is just the sweetest thing."

"Please don't start bawling, Betty," Eunice said. Turning toward us, she did a dramatic eye roll. "We're working our way through them, but with this one caterwauling over every *I love you like the moon loves the stars* or other such malarkey, we are not getting very far."

"In those days the words were poetic and heartfelt," Betty said. "You have not one romantic bone in your body, Eunice. If you did, you'd appreciate the days of chivalry and gentlemanly behavior."

"I'm waiting to hear more scandal. Intrigue.

Suspense. Family secrets exposed. Downton Abbey sort of stuff."

"That sounds like you, Eunice!" Ruth called out from across the hall. And we all started laughing.

"Seriously though, you all are tackling a daunting task," Hannah said. "And I really appreciate it."

Ruth admonished her gals. "My friend Eleanor is entrusting you with valuable information. If you find scandals or questionable family history, well, I guess be considerate. We all have a few of those things in our past, too." Ruth's eyes flicked toward me before turning back to the photographs spread out in front of her.

My next stop was the Whitlow Bed and Breakfast. The Whitlow B&B was a classic beauty. Kay had done a terrific job bringing out the Victorian splendor by balancing the gray-blue body with white trim and vivid russet accents. The ornate detail on the railings and posts was eye-catching and in perfect proportion.

Kay greeted me warmly and welcomed me in. Halls were lined with historic framed photographs. When I mentioned the photograph Todd spoke of, she knew just where to take me.

The image captured us at but one moment in time. I leaned against Dad's leg. He rested his hand on my shoulder, pulling me in close as I looked up at him laughing. I appeared to be about nine years old. Mom stood on his other side, her eyes directed at the photographer. I was wearing one of the special outfits she liked to dress me in. Who took it? Maybe Aunt Ruth?

"Where did you find this?" I asked Kay.

"The photograph was here among several things left by the Bell family. I searched them out, but none of their descendants seemed to care about old photos left behind. Guess it just wasn't their bag. I hope someday they might stay here as guests and see what I've done with the place."

"I hope they do too. Did you know this was my hometown? This picture is of me and my mother and father in front of our family business. I don't have a memory of the Bell family who lived in this house so I'm not sure why they'd have this."

"I love that photo. I knew it was of the studio on Main Street, but I had no idea of that connection to you until Saturday when Jeff was explaining it to me at your grand opening. And I just love your Aunt Ruth. Such a pleasant woman."

"I know it might be a lot to ask, but could I borrow this and make a copy for myself? And maybe one for the collection at the Harmony Museum as well."

"Sure, go ahead. I'm glad you heard about it and enjoyed seeing it." She took the framed photograph down and handed it to me.

"My friend Todd told me how you pamper your guests. Are you from this area?"

"No, I wish. I'm originally from Milwaukee. Restoring an old Victorian house was something I got into my head to do. My mother always said I was an old soul, even as a child. I'm one of five children. Two still live in the Milwaukee area where my parents are. The oldest has retired to Florida. The youngest is still in the Navy."

"How did you find this place?"

"I searched real estate guides online for properties and Pinterest for ideas. I kept expanding how far I searched. I knew I wanted to stay in the Midwest but be in a small town. This place was just right. And the bed-and-breakfast part of this grew out of my friends following my restoration progress and suggesting I open up to guests. So here I am."

"And Todd was so glad he found you."

"I love that he felt pampered here. I enjoy that part of this whole thing more than I imagined. In fact, today I'm taking one of my guests over to Portage to catch the 7:10 Amtrak train. It's a service I offer the guests. I've had many guests who've arrived and left that way. The train makes for an easy getaway, especially from Chicago. Once you're in Harmony, everything is in easy walking distance."

"That's a great idea. Is your guest from Chicago?"

"Yes. He is here on business. Kind of a loner, but he's in terrific physical shape, rides his bike everywhere, especially the Go Round Trail."

"I walked that path Monday night. Quite a project. Who was this Mary person that it's named after?"

"Funny you should ask. Mary's last name was Bell."

"What? She lived in this house?"

Kay nodded. "Small world. Mary understood the value of outdoor physical exercise and was ahead of her time in encouraging it in others. Come with me, I'll show you a photograph I have of her."

Mary Bell's black-and-white photograph was taken with this house in the background. It showed her dressed in trousers with a stylish tailored jacket. She held the handlebars of a bicycle and what looked like a Springer spaniel lay at her feet.

"Jackie, I love to give my guests information about local attractions. Remember my suggestion that I exhibit some of your photographs here? Might help tourists find you."

"Yes. Of course. It's an excellent idea and I appreciate it. If there's a way I can return the favor, please let me know," I said.

My phone text signal went off. It was Patti. She was ready to meet at the old farm.

"Sorry Kay, but I have to leave. I really appreciate you lending me this photograph of my family. I'll get it back to you ASAP."

"Wait a minute. Let me wrap it and put it in a bag for you." Kay returned shortly with a small handled gift bag with her B&B logo on it.

"You think of everything."

Kay laughed. "I put these in the guest rooms with brochures and such in them, which I left in for protective padding. Now if you ever have a flier made up, I'll include it as well. Bye now. Nice to have spent some time with you, Jackie."

CHAPTER TWENTY

When I stopped by the studio to pick up Libby, Mandy called me over to meet two couples. Turns out they were guests from Kay's bed-and-breakfast.

"I just left there," I said. "I hope you're enjoying your stay in Harmony."

"We are. It's a lovely town and we try to get here at least once a year. We are having Mandy frame one of your prints and ship it to a friend in Los Angeles. I'll be sure to let him know we were privileged to meet you."

Mandy said, "Jackie, if these friendly people don't mind, I'd like to take a photograph of them with you to use on our social media."

"We'd love to!" All four said at once.

Mandy arranged us next to the print they'd chosen.

She insisted Libby be included. After a quick couple of photographs, I excused myself. I'd have to remember to thank Mandy for suggesting that.

*T*he farm looked different entering from the road. The driveway was evident by two tire tracks with low grasses growing up in between them. The property was overgrown with gangly shrubs and long tall grasses.

Patti's car sat near the weathered gray farmhouse. A weary-looking place... tired of being beaten against by winter snows and faded by the summer sun.

As soon as I parked next to Patti's car, Libby jumped out. She began bouncing around, her tail wagging above the grasses as she ran, sniffing all the country smells. Her head and mine both popped up when we heard a loud metallic screech.

There it was again.

A rhythmic sound, like an old swing chain.

I poked my head around the corner of the house and saw Patti throwing her weight behind the rhythmic up and down motion required to bring water up to the bucket resting under the pump's spigot.

Libby got to her first. Patti stopped pumping to greet her. "Hey there, Libby!"

"That looks like hard work," I said. "Wouldn't it be easier to turn on a faucet?"

"Very funny!" She stood and arched her back in a slow stretch. "Keeps my arms strong, but it's starting to do a number on my back." The water sloshed out over the edges of the blue plastic pail and onto Patti's short rubber boots as she moved it to a second bucket sitting in a child's wooden wagon.

"Welcome to my quiet little corner of the world. This is my happy place."

"That's how Mandy described it. I can see why. What a charming place."

"You should have seen it when Grandma had chickens and pigs. They still used horses to do the farm work when I was young. Eventually progress found us and Grandpa got an Allis Chalmers tractor. I've had a garden here now for about five years. Like I said, this is a soothing, meditative time for me. Let me roll these on over to the garden and then show you around the place. Want to see inside the house while you're here?"

"Absolutely."

"There's still many of the old family things in there. I guess none of us remaining family members want to let go of it. We watched our grandparents grow old here."

"Bet it was hard for them to face the fact that they would be the last generation to farm this land," I said.

"It was…and too hard for us to empty the place and sell. Obviously! Because we haven't," she said. "It'll probably take our children or grandchildren to do it, eventually."

Her garden was enormous. At least to this city girl's eyes. Patti planted it on the southern sunny side of the house where old clothes lines still hung suspended between tilting metal posts. The laundry long gone, but a mildewy bag holding wooden clothes pins still hung over the line.

I helped pour water over the thirsty plants, around potato mounds, and under wire teepees that would soon have bean plants growing up them.

Inside the house, a haunting feeling arose. I felt the presence of the family who lived here. When she said many things were left, she wasn't exaggerating.

A red and white checked apron hung on a hook next to the white enamel sink. Gently touching it, Patti said, "This was my grandmother's favorite." She ran her fingers along the edge of the blue enamel cook stove. "We'd dry our mittens here when we came in from sledding."

Much of the furniture was gone, but a few random pieces remained. Enough to show which room had been the proper parlor at one time, but now held only a broken legged side chair, a standing lamp, and a carved back settee with large rips in its cushion. These had probably been prized possessions for this family at one time.

We made our way to an enclosed staircase leading to the second story bedrooms.

Patti pointed out a small room at the top of the stairs. "This one had a bed with a feather mattress in it for the grandchildren to sleep in when we stayed," Patti said. "Grandma would let us sleep out on the front porch too, and sometimes even in the hayloft if we were feeling adventurous. From this tiny window we could see this entire side of the farm, the orchards, the barn, the machine shed, and the wooded hills far out beyond our little world here."

I went to enjoy the view she was describing. I slipped the thin curtain to one side, sneezing at the dust that rose up.

"Patti, do you ever drive your car around the back here?" I pointed out the smashed grass tracks I saw from my vantage point. "It looks like someone has."

"No, I don't. And I don't know of anyone who would have. Do you mind if we go down and take a look at those? I didn't notice anything when I was here on Sunday afternoon, but then I might not have seen them from where I work in the garden. And I probably wouldn't have noticed them if we hadn't come up here.

Hope some kids haven't discovered the place and started using it as party central. Having raves, waves, whatever they call them in the machine shed!"

The tracks led between the farm's outbuildings. We each walked in one of paths created by car tires, following them around to the backside of what Patti pointed out was a machine shed when we came upon what had made the tracks.

A big sedan was parked tight against the wall of the shed. An old wooden door, several dead shrubs, and a rolled-up snow fence leaned against the vehicle in an attempt to camouflage it.

CHAPTER TWENTY-ONE

It shocked me. This was the car that had an all-points bulletin issued on it, Alan Morris's car. We stood there with our mouths hanging open for a few seconds before Patti started pulling the large dead branches away.

"How dare someone just leave their car here on my property?"

"Wait. We'd better not move or touch anything."

"Why not? It's an abandoned car. Nice one, though. Why would someone just junk it here?"

I peeked in the windows. No dead body. An edginess descended. Was someone watching us? There were so many places to hide. Was that a movement behind the slightly ajar barn door? Did the bedroom curtain just move? There, in the orchard, cracking branches? Footsteps?

Patti stared me. "What's wrong, Jackie?"

"Patti, the people who left this car might be long gone or very close. I don't know which," I said. "Are you okay?"

"I'm okay, just angry. I want to face the person who did this."

She was probably right. I overreacted. This car had been here awhile. Someone didn't just drive it over before I got here. Calm down Jackie, I told myself. You need to think clearly.

"Look, Patti. I'd like you to stay here while I go to town. I'll be back later. Do you feel safe?"

"Safe? Yes. Why shouldn't I? Don't worry about me. I'll stay until you come back. But what are you going to do?"

"First, I'm going to let Jeff know about us finding Alan's car."

Patti's eyes flew open. "This is the dead guy's car?"

"Yes. We don't have a good cell phone signal here, so I'm going to drive to town and let Jeff know. Maybe you should come with me."

"No way. I'm alright. Just caught me by surprise. Now I'm getting my angry back," Patti said. She crossed her arms over her chest to make her point.

"Is there access to that opening I see up in the barn?" I asked.

"To the hayloft? There was last time I looked."

"If anyone comes, except me, hide yourself. They might be dangerous. Don't try to stand your ground. Promise?"

"I promise. But what about my car? They'd see it."

"Can you drive it into one of these buildings?"

Patti's eyes darted around before landing on a lean-to attached to the barn. "We used that for firewood. It's been empty since Grandma insisted on a furnace. I can drive it in there. No one coming from the road would see it."

I didn't want to tell her they might not approach from the road, but the greater odds were that the person who parked Alan's car here didn't expect it to be found for years. And wouldn't be planning on returning here today. At least not yet.

*B*ack in Harmony, I immediately went to the police station.

"You have got to be kidding! You found the car we've all been looking for? I need to see this right away. We'll get it fingerprinted and searched. There are sure to be some clues in it as Alan obviously didn't park it there himself," Jeff said. "This is a big break. My first thoughts go toward Tony because he would know those back roads and the places that are long abandoned. I figured that's how he got in on Sunday. He came in the back way and hid his car. Waited until Rick was alone and killed him. Then he got caught in the act when Alan returned to the construction trailer. So, he kills him and dumps the body in the excavated hole."

I, however, didn't think the case wrapped up quite that neatly. "But Jeff..."

Jeff held up his hand as though afraid he would lose his train of thought. "I know there are pieces that don't fit in this narrative. But he is now my number one suspect for Rick's murder. Plus, it fits perfectly with what Scott told me. How the guys said Tony wasn't supposed to even be working at that spot. If you hadn't been watching drone footage, he'd have covered up the body better. No one would have found it."

"Maybe, but it all seems so complicated."

"Not if you strip it down to motive and opportunity. He had a motive. Rick was hitting on Laura."

"No, he wasn't," I quickly added.

"You have to think like the murderer. He thought Rick was, and that's all that matters. He had the opportunity. He snuck in on the back road, knowing Rick would be working on Sunday evening. Alan was in the wrong place at the wrong time is all. He messed up the entire plan."

"Do you have the video of Alan's car leaving the site on Sunday in your computer? If you could pull it up for me, I'd like to take another look at it."

I was still trying to catch the thread of what kept slipping away on me. I needed something to grab hold of and pull at.

Tony. The scene I witnessed at Stone Mill. My thoughts about him and Laura. That night at Shorty's. The sun glinting off something far away on the construction site. Tony pushing dirt on top of Alan's body.

Had Tony come back and waited until we all left the construction trailer like Jeff thinks? Had he lain in wait to catch Rick alone? Did Alan go back up to the construction trailer after I left and walk into the middle of a murder scene?

"Here you go Jackie, I have the gate video up."

I walked around to lean over Jeff's shoulder and saw the grainy image of Alan's car leave through the gate. The time of the tape when Alan's car left was almost an hour after I did. He seemed in a hurry. Why? To get on the road to Chicago?

"If you're determined to charge Tony, can you please give me just an hour before you go out to arrest him?"

"Look Jackie, I don't know all of what happened, but I'll wait to arrest. He's not a flight risk."

"Could I have one of those large envelopes? The ones with the clasp on them?"

"Sure," Jeff said, handing me one from the file cabinet behind him.

"Oh, and don't go up to the farm just yet. The car isn't going anywhere. Wait for a call within the hour with further directions. If you don't get one, go ahead to the farm. Deal?"

"What are you up to? Don't put yourself in danger like you did with that Luella murder."

"Me? Never."

On my way out to the resort job site, I made a couple of phone calls. My time was limited.

CHAPTER TWENTY-TWO

I entered the sales office, asking Kim if she could put promotional papers in the envelope I handed her. "And I need to see Laura. Is she around?"

"She ran some paperwork up to Scott at the construction trailer. Is there something I can help you with?"

"Oh darn. I was hoping I could talk to her before the police come."

"Police? What's up, Jackie?" Kim asked. "Are they coming to question her about something? That poor girl. She's been through so much this week. Another fight with Tony. I wish she'd dump the bum."

"Can I tell you this in confidence, Kim?"

"Oh, I love intrigue. Is there a breakthrough in the

investigation? More clues? A mysterious new character?"

"Kim, nothing so exciting sounding. But for Laura, a very upsetting turn of events. Chief Jeff will be here shortly to arrest Tony for the murder of Rick Ballard."

Kim's hand flew to her mouth. "Wow. How did they figure that out?"

"Short version. He was here on the site Sunday night and waited until Rick was alone in the trailer. He knew about the handgun Rick kept in his desk and made it look like a suicide."

"What about Alan?" Kim asked.

"They are building a case to prove he killed Alan as well. Laura gave Tony a false alibi. She might be charged with obstruction of justice."

The door to the sales office burst open. Rocco Montalvo exploded into the small space.

Kim and I both spun to look at him.

"Sorry ladies. Bad manners. I didn't mean to startle you," Rocco said. "Is Winford in his office? I have to see him immediately."

"Winford," Kim called. "There's someone to see you."

Rocco didn't wait, but instead stepped brusquely across the room to the accountant's office door.

"Mr. Montalvo, what a pleasant surprise," we heard Winford say. "Can I help you with something?"

"I just received news that the investors' visit has been moved up to tomorrow morning. In fact, they may come to town later tonight and want to meet with you and me as soon as possible."

"What is making you so upset?" Winford asked.

"They are expecting me to have some information that Alan had. He told them if anything happened to him, they were to open an envelope he would give me. But he never gave it to me. I only just learned about it this morning. Now I must find the packet. It has my name on the front. Please tell me he left it with you, Winford."

"He didn't. We went over some things verbally. I assume I can let you know some of what he shared about Rick Ballard ordering inferior products and billing them to the company at full price. Rick's been skimming like that for months. I am only recently coming to understand the depths of it."

"Winford, I suspected as much. Alan knew about Rick and shared that with you. The packet must contain other incriminating information."

"But sir, that's why I'm here. I've compiled data to that end. And you'll be able to show your investors that. Trust me, it's quite complete."

"You're probably right. I suspect Alan kept an unassuming folder as a backup. Nothing that would pique someone's interest. I gained access to his motel cottage and could find nothing. But the place looked like it had been ransacked."

"Sir, what is it you're asking me to do?"

"Well, a start would be to find his car," Rocco snapped. "I imagine that's where he kept the file. With him at all times."

"Of course, but the authorities could not locate it."

"Winford, I need to make sure that it doesn't fall into the wrong hands. Alan was ready to reveal these things this weekend. Now he's dead, and what might be incriminating evidence is out there somewhere."

"Incriminating who, sir?" Winford asked.

"Just find it!" Rocco shouted before he stomped out of the room and left the office.

Winford stepped out and stared after him.

Kim cleared her throat. "Well now. That was interesting. Jackie and I couldn't help but overhear the conversation. I've never seen Mr. Montalvo so upset. I could keep my eyes open around here for the folder and ask Scott about looking in the construction trailer."

"That sounds like a good idea," Winford said. "This is all so upsetting. I know the investors were concerned about cost overruns and possible mishandling of monies, but Alan's having something secretive sounding is confusing. Do you think Mr. Montalvo is in trouble? He seemed very shook up."

"I'm very shook up," Kim said. "This is all just getting to be too much. I wanted to have some promotional material ready for the investors' group. Now they're coming early. If it isn't one thing, it's another. I find a dead body. You find a dead body, Jackie. There can't be more that can go wrong."

I picked up the envelope from Kim's desk. "I'll help you with these promotional things. I talk a good game. Plus I could sketch up a couple of ideas that would help flush out your presentation. Though it sounds like they might have bigger fish to fry tomorrow."

"Sure, let's get together later. Winford, will you be ready for the meeting tomorrow? These guys springing a surprise like this is quite rude and inconsiderate. I just hope you don't have to stay late tonight."

"I'm actually in pretty good shape with my financial papers. In fact, I may leave early today. Sounds like tomorrow will be busy."

CHAPTER TWENTY-THREE

I'd made one last call before I got into the hills.

Patti's gardening chores were finished when I got back to the farm. I didn't get to let her know what had happened while I was gone. And I was glad she didn't ask a lot of questions as I hid my car around the corner of the house.

I put the envelope I'd brought to Kim's office in the back seat of Alan's abandoned car.

"Why are you doing that?" Patti asked.

"Hopefully you'll see why soon."

The ladder up to the hayloft had seen better days. Patti went first, gingerly putting her weight on each rung. She looked back down at me. "They built them to last one hundred years. I don't feel any give. Come on up." And the last thing I saw was her bright red gardening boots disappear over the edge of the large square opening.

"Wait a minute, this farm is over a hundred years old, isn't it?" I called up.

Her head appeared back in the opening. "Did I say one hundred? I meant two hundred."

"Very funny." I adjusted my camera case on my shoulder and began climbing up. The telephoto lens made the case heavier, and it banged against me as I climbed.

Getting off the ladder, I crawled on the rough raw floorboards a few feet before standing. This loft was huge. Heavy roughhewn timbers spanned the width of the structure. Motes, stirred by our movement, danced in the sunlight coming through the wall cracks. Dry earthy smells hung in the air. Patti's silhouette was stark against the bright sunlight outside the open loft door.

"Now we wait. If I'm right, someone will arrive shortly." I placed my camera on an old wooden crate. I'd be shooting at a distance, so I preferred not doing hand-held shots.

"And if you're wrong?" Patti asked.

"Then we go back to Harmony."

"Why the hiding? Is the person dangerous?"

"Could be. I'm just not sure." I proceeded to tell Patti about the scene on the dock at the Stone Mill months ago. And how I'd misjudged reactions.

"Things spun unexpectedly. I wasn't prepared. It turned out okay, but that was thanks to a couple of friends. One of them was your ex, Scott."

"Scott? What was he doing there?"

"The area was still under construction and I think he was checking it out as a builder himself."

"He's a nice guy. I've always hoped he'd find someone after we divorced. I carry some guilt around with me about that whole situation."

"The divorce was amicable?"

"It was. But I just wish for him to find someone again. I believe he is afraid to trust again, to put himself out. That age-old fear trying and losing again."

I sensed something and quickly put a finger to my lips. Squatting back in the shadows of the barn, I whispered, "We need to be still now. I'm going to my camera to take some photos. Just stay here out of sight."

Patti nodded.

I watched the figure walking out of the woods.

He snuck toward the farm.

Through the telephoto lens, I watched his eyes darting right and left.

I took a deep breath and released it... much as a

hunter will do before pulling the trigger. I began shooting.

CHAPTER TWENTY-FOUR

A dark sedan was parked on Oak Street near the Whitlow Bed and Breakfast. Patti and I had pulled over well down the block. We watched.

It was a tense few minutes until we saw Kay come out of the house carrying a suitcase and put it in the back seat of her vehicle. Another figure came around the side yard pushing a bike. He lifted it, putting it on the bike rack attached to Kay's car.

Two men stepped out of the dark sedan and approached Kay and exchanged a few words as Winford Tarver strapped his bike down. Then Patti and I watched as Chief Jeff waved us over.

Winford's confident look faded when he saw me approaching. Jeff noticed his sudden change in demeanor and asked him to put both hands on the vehicle.

"What is this about, officer?" Winford said, while Murph patted him down.

"Let's take a seat here and have a chat," Jeff said, pointing to the front porch steps.

Winford was the only one who sat down.

"Mr. Tarver, we're placing you under arrest for the murder of Alan Morris," Jeff said.

"What on earth are you talking about? I didn't kill anyone." Winford started to stand.

"Please sir, remain seated," Jeff said.

"Why are these women standing here staring at me?"

Jeff stood looking down at Winford. "They have some information to share with us. Let's start with you explaining how you knew where Mr. Morris's vehicle was?"

The look on Winford's face was priceless. He knew where he had just come from, but he was trying to process how any of us would know. Finally, in a hesitant voice, he said, "I have no idea where that vehicle is. Why would you think that?"

"Jackie, could you bring your camera here please?" Jeff said. "I believe Mr. Tarver's memory might be refreshed by seeing those photographs you just took at the Woller farm."

"Sure, I'd be happy too." The camera hanging around my neck contained evidence that would eventually be used in court. I'd never experienced that kind of weight before. I lifted the strap over my head and pulled up the stored photos before passing it to Jeff. "Just click this small arrow to advance the photographs. The first one is when I caught sight of him coming out of the edge of the forest. There are quite a few shots, but I think you'll get to an image that will better remind him where he just came from. And I believe you will find the envelope you see him removing from Alan Morris's automobile in his luggage."

Winford waved away the camera. The crushing look of defeat took over his entire body. He slumped down, looking at the ground. "I have experienced this temptation before."

"What temptation is that, Mr. Tarver?" I asked.

"So many schemes I've uncovered. White collar fraud. They hide the money away, maybe even get caught, but only stay in a country club prison a few months. Then they leave and enjoy the wealth they cheated to get. To slip a small amount from the funds that pass across the books I handle, what would it matter to them?"

He looked up. When no one offered a reply, he continued. "But I never did. Until now."

Jeff read Winford his Miranda rights as he hand-cuffed him.

"How'd you find the car?" he asked.

"You thought that farm was abandoned. You thought you were safe to leave it there. It would slowly rust away," I said. "But that farm belongs to a friend of mine. Meet Patti Woller. It was on her family farm that you went one more time. And we knew you were coming."

Winford looked up at me. "It was that Rocco guy. He was part of this setup, wasn't he? There was no important package hidden somewhere, was there?"

"That's right," I said.

"But what makes you think it was me who killed Alan and hid the car?"

"Your potential involvement in this has been hovering at the edges of my curious mind since Sunday. I overheard you in the meeting at the construction trailer, but I didn't see you. When Rick Ballard's body was discovered, and the police blood spatter report ruled out suicide, you weren't a suspect."

"Are you saying that now I am being charged with Rick's murder as well? The first charge is crazy and now you're just way out in left field. Today you even told Laura that Tony was going to be arrested for Rick's death. I heard you."

The look on his face was priceless when he realized

the whole thing, including both Rocco's performance and my conversation with Kim was a setup to fool him.

"I didn't do it. I was being blackmailed and the person doing it told me where to find the car. To get that package for him."

Jeff said, "Now we're getting somewhere. I think Tony may have murdered Rick."

"Jeff, I'm certain you'll find Winford's fingerprints inside the vehicle proving he drove it away, not Tony's. But first, Kay, would you be so kind as to bring out those discarded clothes you found in the garbage?"

Kay nodded and walked into the house.

"We have the physical proof we need to convict you of Alan's murder. But showing you shot and killed Rick will be proved as well."

Kim returned and handed a large zip-lock bag containing clothing to Jeff.

"A young man lurked on the construction site Sunday night. He was waiting to confront Rick about messing with his girlfriend. He said Rick was already dead when he got there. That the lights were on, but the door was locked. Which meant either Rick locked it and killed himself, or the killer had a key and locked it when he left."

"I don't have a key to the construction trailer," Winford announced, as though this vindicated him.

"You didn't. But Alan did. On Sunday, I interrupted a heated meeting. I left, but Rick, you, and Alan remained behind. That night the sales office had no lights on. When Kim arrived the next morning, she noticed lights on."

"So?" Winford snipped.

"I believe you knew that Alan and the investors he represented were closing in on Rick. And that made you vulnerable as well, didn't it Winford? Things were spiraling out of control. Today when Rocco announced the investors were coming in earlier than expected, you panicked and changed your plans to leave this afternoon instead of tomorrow."

I pulled a paper out of my back pocket and handed it to Jeff. "I think you'll be interested to know that the Amtrak train Kay was scheduled to take him to on Friday was not heading to Chicago. The Empire Builder was coming out of Chicago and heading west. I would think leaving today he'd also have chosen a west-bound train."

Kay looked stunned. "How did you know that?"

"Nice gift bag you gave me, including all the information about the area. It also had the Amtrak schedule in it."

"None of this explains me killing either man."

"Oh, but it does. The clothing in the bag Murph is

holding will have Rick's blood on it, from when you shot him in the construction trailer. First you killed Alan, probably while he was putting your bike in the trunk of his car to give you a ride home. Perhaps the coroner will find a sharp-edged blow to Alan's neck that came from you slamming the trunk lid down on him before slipping his body into the trunk. Or maybe you quarreled in the office and knocked him out there. But now you had a dilemma. Rick wouldn't go for this part of the crooked scheme you two were running. When you went back to the construction trailer, you and he argued. You knew he kept a gun in his desk. Everyone did. You got to it and shot him, wiped it clean, put Rick's prints on it, and left. But now you had a body to get rid of. I surmised you took Alan's car back through the site, found a pit, and buried him in a shallow grave. I'm sure you hoped they would pour concrete over him. And if not, no problem. No one would even look for him out on the construction site. Then you put your bike in the trunk and drove out through the gate."

"Oh man, Jackie," Jeff said. "You mean when we saw Alan's car leaving the site on Sunday, this guy was driving it?"

"Exactly. It would send everyone scattering, thinking Alan had left for Chicago. He even took on Alan's limp at the Riverview and went into his cottage, knowing how cameras are so prevalent."

Patti stuck her face close to Winford's. "Except at old farms where he could ditch the car and no security camera to record it. Take his bike out and catch the trail back to the B&B. Quite a crooked scheme you hatched. You're no dummy."

"But what is in the bag Kay gave me?" Jeff asked.

"Now here is where Winford wasn't thinking clearly. He imagined the bloodied clothing he threw in the trash, which is now in that bag you're holding, would be hauled away. And one other clue that fell into place on Monday was a remark by another guest here. He noticed that your shoes, which you always took off at the door, were covered with red clay soil Monday morning. The murders occurred Sunday night. That was a particularly careless mistake."

Jeff grinned. "I'm headed up to the car right after this guy is booked. I thought I was only going to be looking for fingerprints. But I'll be sure to check the trunk for evidence as well. Nice job, Jackie."

Neighbors were stopping to watch. Curtains parted in nearby windows. This was quite a sight on Oak Street on a Thursday afternoon.

More attention was drawn to the whole tableau when Kim came racing up in her big white SUV with her realtor logo on the door and her husband Stuart in tow. As soon as she screeched to a halt Stuart popped out with his wife close behind.

"Woot toot. We did it, Jackie. It worked." Kim shouted. "I told you so, Stuart. I told you, didn't I?"

Stuart beamed at his wife. "You sure did, honey."

"We conspired together and..." Kim pointed at the pathetic figure sitting on the porch steps. "The criminal is caught. Did I do good, Jackie? It was so exciting to be part of this trap you laid. Here, Stu take a picture of me with the murderer behind me. Jackie, come over here too. And get him being handcuffed in the background."

Jeff stepped in. "Kim, not right now, please. We need to get Winford booked at the station."

"Sure, Chief. I understand these things, you know. I've been a part of several cases now," Kim said, adjusting her collar. "Stu honey, just a quick shot of whatever you can get. Maybe you'll use it for tomorrow's paper."

Stuart took several cell phone photographs. He pulled Patti aside to ask her some questions. She rolled her eyes at me but took her time telling Stuart what she knew.

Jeff directed Officer Murphy to take Winford to the station for booking.

"Kay, how did you know to call me?" Jeff asked.

"Jackie called right after leaving Kim's office, with directions. She let me know that Winford would be bicycling by, based on the scene at the sales office. I walked up to the cemetery gate and pretended I was fussing with the flowers on a grave there. My direction was to call you when I saw him pedaling past. He was in a big hurry."

"And that's also when I asked Kay to dumpster dive and see if Winford ditched his blood-spattered clothes in the trash," I said. "She found the discarded garments."

"Jackie, why not just let me know about him coming out to the farm? We could have trapped him there," Jeff asked me.

"I thought it was him, but I needed proof, which I got through my camera lens. There's no cell signal out there. I expected him to return here and ask Kay to take him to the train right away today. So, Kay reached out to you to wait and make the arrest here."

"What if things went wrong at the farm? You promised you wouldn't put yourself in danger," Jeff said.

"Patti and I were safely hidden in a spot where I could focus my camera on him and catch him in the act. And it worked. I didn't put us in danger. I knew he was planning to leave town early, ahead of the investors Rocco said were coming tomorrow or maybe were on their way already. I figured he'd want to get out of here as soon as possible."

"Was that envelope you took from my office the bait for the trap you were laying out for Winford?"

I had to grin. "Yes. I owe you an envelope."

"You don't owe me a thing, except a more thorough explanation of how you put this all together."

"I'll explain later, Jeff. I need a shower. Crawling around in a hay loft leaves me itchy all over."

"Okay, I'll hold you to that," Jeff said. "Kay, could you show me Winford's room? I'd like to do a quick search of it." I caught the wink Jeff gave me as he followed Kay into the house.

Patti came over to tell me she had to head back into the village hall, but that she had enjoyed our rather unusual afternoon together.

Stuart caught a shot of Murph holding Winford Tarver's head down as he placed him in the back seat of his cruiser. He'd be working late tonight to get tomorrow's paper out.

CHAPTER TWENTY-FIVE

s I left the Whitlow B&B, I made a phone call to Rocco to let him know things had gone as planned. When he suggested a lobster dinner at the Wildwood Supper Club, I said, "I was thinking hot dogs and fries at the Harbor Dogs, but lobster does sound lovely. Let me drop Libby off and take a quick shower."

"I look forward to hearing the rest of your story, Jacqueline, especially since you included me in your caper," Rocco said.

The Wildwood was busy for a Thursday evening. Rocco was chatting with Lynn, the bartender. Always a lady's man, I thought.

"Hello Jacqueline. I'm delighted you could join me. My dear Lynn, please set this fine lady up with whatever cocktail she desires."

"Hey Jackie," Lynn said. "Your regular?"

"That sounds great Lynn, thanks."

"You have a regular drink?" Rocco asked.

I smiled and said, "Here I do. I ordered my aunt's favorite, a whiskey old-fashioned sweet one evening, and whenever I come here, it seems like the perfect thing. Very Wisconsinish, don't you think?"

"I will try one of those myself," Rocco said.

As soon as Lynn put our drinks in front of us, Rocco said, "Now Jacqueline, please let us toast to your most recent success. Cheers to trapping a murderer."

"Cheers, Rocco. I couldn't have done it without you!"

We were soon escorted to our river view table where the traditional relish waited. After we placed our dinner order, we got down to talking about what happened today.

Rocco said, "You were in such a hurry when you called requesting my presence at The Hills sales office that I feared I might fail in what you expected of me."

"I'm thankful you trusted me, Rocco. And I do owe you an explanation. First, may I compliment you on your acting skills. I was very impressed!"

"Thank you, Jacqueline. I've had to use them more that once in my career. There was that time in a New Jersey back alley that was rather sketchy, but enough about me. I would very much enjoy hearing the backstory to what led you to accuse Winford Tarver as Alan Morris's murderer."

"And possibly Rick Ballard's murderer as well."

Rocco stopped his drink midair. "Well now, that's an interesting twist. Please go on."

"The heated discussion between Rick, Alan, and Winford that I overheard on Sunday was troubling. I didn't know Winford at the time, but I'd met Rick and certainly knew Alan Morris. Alan became a suspect in Rick's death and couldn't be reached. Dropping off the face of the earth, like he was guilty. Then the police's attention shifted to a young man at the site. He had motive and opportunity as well. He thought Rick was hitting on his girlfriend."

"Ah, the love triangle and what passion will make a man do," Rocco said.

"I have to agree with you. That was what Kim and I were talking about before you got to the office today. I wanted Winford to overhear us and relax, thinking he wasn't in anyone's radar for either of the murders."

"However, even that conversation with Kim was acting, and by this time Winford was in your radar?"

"Right. Remember, on Sunday I did that Mary's Go Round trail and saw you at the marina? My walk also took me past Whitlow's Bed and Breakfast, where a friend was staying. I saw him and stopped to chat. He told me an odd fact about seeing another guest, who seemed so fastidious, returning with shoes covered in a reddish soil. Just an offhand comment."

"Your curiosity was piqued?"

"Not right then. Todd and I chuckled about it, and that was all. Remember, I didn't know Winford at this time. I didn't tie the man I'd heard on Sunday with some fussy guest at a B&B. Seeing Alan's car hidden where it was today, and seeing where his body was found, this innocent remark on Monday became a clue. And the whole thing snapped into place."

"Please, there has to be more," Rocco said.

"There is, but first let's enjoy our dinner," I said as our waitress arrived with lobsters and twice-baked potatoes, temporarily shifting our conversation to trips we'd each taken to Maine and the lobster boils there. The meal was delicious and the ambiance perfect.

We each ordered an after-dinner coffee.

"Jacqueline, I've been thinking about what you've told me so far, and it doesn't get me to Winford's motive," Rocco said.

"Earlier today I visited Kay Whitlow, owner of the B&B I mentioned earlier. She talked about taking a guest, who I learned was Winford Tarver, to the Amtrak station earlier than expected. My mind goes, hmm... that must be the man with the reddish soil on his shoes that Todd told me about. This morning I'd seen that type of soil where Alan's body was unearthed."

"But Jacqueline, significant portions of that site exhibit similar soil makeup."

"Yes, but patience, Rocco. These are clues more easily explained looking back at them. Discovering Alan's car was a big one. Found at a place discoverable from the bike trail Winford took daily. On the night of Rick's murder, Alan was planning on putting the bike in his trunk and driving Winford to the B&B because it was so dark out. Now Rocco, imagine a heated argument in the sales office. Winford has been on the take as well."

"What? That's unbelievable. He's a trusted accountant the investor group has used for years," Rocco said.

"When arrested today, he told the officers this was the first time. That he just watched people making money, and sometimes fraudulently. He finally succumbed to the temptation."

"I'm glad I wasn't the one who hired him," Rocco said. "I'm in shock, but you are making a strong case, Jacqueline. Your premise gives me his motive, to silence others who know about his unlawful deeds. But now please share how he accomplished this."

"My theory on what happened after I left them

Sunday evening is that he killed Alan at the sales office. Kay Whitlow mentioned that he was in good physical shape from all the biking he did."

Rocco chuckled. "His office demeanor and dress did not reveal the physicality of him. Winford would have had the strength to move a body out of a car trunk, a dead weight. Difficult."

"Bingo!"

"Question, please. Why not just leave Alan in the trunk and still just hide the car, body in the trunk and all?"

"He knew about the camera at the gate. It's obvious. Body out of trunk and bike in, drive through the gate, and mission accomplished. Everyone would think it was Alan leaving."

"Ah yes." Rocco nodded his head and leaned forward on his elbows. "And I suppose the age-old fear of getting caught driving with a dead man in your trunk."

I grinned. "There's that too! Anyway, he drove to the motel and appeared on the camera there, faking Alan's limp, reinforcing the idea of Alan picking something up before he drove back to Chicago."

"Now I see. This was a simple, but effective trick to buy him time. Everyone was fooled into thinking Alan had left. Then Winford drove the car to the spot he already knew about, got his bike out, and rode back to the B&B in the dark."

"With those dirty shoes," I added.

"And the story you asked me to tell, about the investors coming early and them wanting to see this mysterious envelope Alan had supposedly told them about, would be the final push to send Winford over the edge and end up revealing the car's hiding place. Did you actually put an envelope for him to retrieve in the car?"

"Yes, I did. Kim helped with that. We needed to lure him over there. Only the murderer would know the car was left at the farm. But Winford could have just left without ever going to the car. He had to get his hands on what he suspected might reveal his part in this fraud scheme. I had Kim put together a paper with hand-written numbers, letters, symbols appearing to be pass-words or some sort of code. She stashed a thumb drive in it as well. Clever Kim put the video of the drone flyover on it in case he uploaded it to take a peek."

"That's amusing. A bit of a twisted sense of humor. When the investors arrive this weekend, I will have quite the story to share with them. Thanks to you, Jacqueline."

"Happy to help! And thank you for dinner. I am going home and straight to bed. I've had a full day."

As we left the restaurant and walked through the crowded bar area to leave, I saw Scott seated at the bar.

He didn't notice me, though, he had his back to us and was busy talking to the attractive woman next to him. It wasn't some random thing. They obviously had arrived together.

CHAPTER TWENTY-SIX

Another dream tonight. This was one of hearing the soothing, calming voice of my mother humming softly and staring out her bedroom window of our home on Oak Street, her beauty taking my breath away. I called to her, but she didn't answer or even turn her head. I walked next to her to look out the window. She was staring at a cemetery just below us. I ran downstairs and stood in front the large gate to the cemetery, trying to wave up at Mother. Now she'd see me. For sure she would wave back at her little girl. But she was gone from the window.

My dreams blur lines and rearrange truths. Sometimes so wonderful that I want to stay in them. Other times so awful that I wake to the sound of my own stifled scream.

I woke Friday morning, and my first thought was I needed to show that photograph from Kay to my Aunt Ruth.

My second thought was that the thing licking my face needed to be let out.

After a shower, I went out to Murphy's for coffee and a donut.

I grabbed a Harmony's Happening newspaper from the stand outside the paper's office. Stuart must have worked late into the night.

The chatter in the coffee shop surrounded me as I walked up to the counter.

Can you believe the accountant did it?

Crazy man!

I thought Tony was the guilty one.

Cheating us out of pay!

The bigwigs are coming in today

They better straighten things out

No one seemed to notice me, and I was glad, at least until Grace greeted me and said, "Jackie, we heard the news that the murderer was arrested. And that you were the one who put all the pieces together."

Conversations stopped, and heads turned. I smiled awkwardly at Grace.

She continued. "Murph told us all about last night.

He said Chief Jeff was praising you up and down to the entire town."

"He was? That was nice, but most of what I added sort of fell into my lap. Could I get a cup of coffee and a...?"

"Maple frosted donut. On the house, Jackie!" Grace exclaimed.

Back at the studio, I took my coffee and donut out to the balcony. "Well Libby, just another morning in Harmony."

Val waved up at me as she opened her salon. "Morning neighbor," she said. "You'll be busy today. Everyone will want to hear the story."

"I hope not. I've had enough excitement. Now I want to relax and enjoy the weekend. Maybe take Libby on a walk on the Go Round trail again." That remark got Libby up and bouncing off my leg. "Sorry girl, I need to learn to spell W A L K instead of saying the word without the action you expect."

Val was laughing. "And the deception begins! You dog people. I know, I know, they are your babies. Just like with our kids. We lie about Santa Claus and spell words out so they don't know what we're talking about."

"I swear I will never lie about Santa to Libby."

"That's good to hear! I've got Kim coming in this

morning. I'm sure she'll fill me in on her part in this latest murder. Catch you later, neighbor."

Val disappeared into her salon and I snapped the Harmony Happenings paper open. The article Stuart wrote about yesterday's events hit the high points. He seemed to have gotten much of his storyline from Kim. That was fine with me. I was ready to distance myself from the entire sad state of affairs. Kim told of how she helped me set up the sting operation that led to Winford's arrest and how she had bad feelings about the guy from his first day in the office.

Enough of this, time to get the place opened up. The morning was busy. I caught up on paperwork and worked with the installers of a new POS, point of sale system, which would incorporate Mandy's custom framing and the sale of other photographers' work. Then I had an appointment with a photographer from Des Moines to look over his portfolio for a future exhibition.

A fair number of customers were browsing.

"Probably tourists getting a jump on the weekend," Mandy said. "Let's set up that sign board we used for the gala. I'll get it from the back."

While she was gone, I opened up a conversation with a young couple who'd been admiring one of the photographs of the bluffs on the east side of town. I introduced myself and learned they had a small printing business online and wondered if I licensed my work for small scale distribution like specialty cards, postcards, and stationary. I liked the sound of that, and we exchanged information.

The door chimed, and I turned with a smile to greet the Des Moines photographer. My smile weakened and thinned, but remained frozen on my face. The person who had entered was Scott, with his son Matt, and the woman from last night. They didn't notice me right away. She was as pretty as Scott was handsome.

Mandy came running past me. "Matt, what a wonderful surprise! And Sophia, I didn't know you were in town. I'm so happy you all stopped in. I'll show you around."

"I came into town and surprised Scott. We had a lovely dinner at the Wildwood last night. This morning, I insisted on seeing Parker Photography. Scott's been telling me about this new place and your part in it."

Mandy motioned me over. "This is my boss, Jacqueline Parker. Jackie, I'd like you to meet Sophia Daniels."

Sophia extended her hand to me. "It's so nice to meet you. Scott's been telling me all about you and how you've taken over this family business."

She turned to Mandy and said, "But now Mandy, I

would much prefer you call me Aunt Sophia as you are part of our family now."

It took me a few seconds to put it together. Scott just stood there grinning at me. Waiting to see the recognition on my face that this woman was his sister.

"Let's show her your framing room first," Matt said. The three of them headed to the back.

As soon as they were out of earshot Scott said, "Are you going to say anything?"

"About what, Scott?" I spoke in as nonchalant tone as I could muster.

"About that look on your face. I noticed you leaving the Wildwood with a dapper older gentleman last night."

"That was Rocco Montalvo. You've met him before."

"I know I have. And now you've met the gorgeous woman I was with last night."

"Will she be in town long?"

"A few days. She's sort of the advance person for the antique market that's coming here to Harmony," Scott said.

A man carrying a large leather portfolio was coming through the door. "I have an appointment now, Scott. Will you and Sophia be here when I finish?"

I slipped my hands behind my back and crossed my fingers and waited for his answer.

"We might be. But I have a better idea," Scott said,

with a hopeful smile tugging at his lips. "Would you join us for dinner tonight? I'd like you and Sophia to get to know each other."

"I'd love to."

he End

THE END

Here are a few ways to reach me...I'd love to stay connected!

Please sign up for my monthly newsletter. I'll share things about my life...both personal as Brenda Felber and professionally as my pen name Suzanne Bolden.
Like/follow Suzanne on her Facebook page

If you follow me on these two, you'll be automatically notified when new releases are available.
Bookbub
Amazon Author Central

Check out my website www.suzannebolden.com

Thank you for reading my books. If you enjoyed them, a review is much appreciated!

Katie Murphy Cozy Mystery Series

#1 Pour Decisions

#2 Pick Yar Poison

#3 Raising Spirits

#4 Auld Lang Stein

#5 A Wee Lepre-Con

#6 Paws for a Pint

7 The Elf Did It

#8 Matrimony and Malice

#9 Read Between the Lines